MAVERICK

Satan's Fury MC

L Wilder

Maverick
Satan's Fury MC
Copyright © 2015 L Wilder
Print Edition

Cover Model – Dave Allen
www.facebook.com/daveallenmusicpage

Cover Design – LJ Anderson
www.facebook.com/lj.anderson.33

Editor – Marci Ponce

Book Teasers and Design – Monica Langley Holloway
www.facebook.com/Kustombooks2reviews

Dedication

To my fellow Indie Authors

Self-publication is not for the faint of hearts. It's a difficult, but truly rewarding journey. I have been greatly blessed to have encountered so many wonderful authors who have shown, time and time again, that with a little faith and persistence, you can do anything. Thank you all for your invaluable support. You guys rock!

MAVERICK

My mother used to say that everything happens for a reason. It didn't matter how insignificant or how heart-wrenchingly tragic, she'd say it was just meant to be. She truly believed that if a person was patient enough… looked hard enough… for *long* enough, they'd be able to find their silver lining. Her faith never faltered. Facing difficult times with strength and determination, my loving mother would wait… no matter how long it took. It might have taken her months or even years, but my mother would always be able to find that light shining at the end of the long, dark tunnel.

I say bullshit. There is *no fucking silver lining*. Shit happens. Hard times are just a part of life, like the air we breathe. We have to learn to deal with the hand we are dealt and move the hell on. Yet, every damn time something fucked up happens in my life, I find myself thinking of my mother. If she were still alive, I wonder what she'd have to say about everything that's happened in my life over the last year. Would she be able to find my silver lining? Because, I sure as hell can't.

Chapter 1

MAVERICK

"**D**ON'T RUSH INTO this, Maverick. I know what you're like. Give it some time, brother," Cotton told me. I could see the concern in his penetrating eyes, and it meant a lot to me that he was trying to help. He was a good man… a good President. The brothers of Satan's Fury looked up to him-admired him. We all knew that the club was his life, and he was all about the brotherhood. As our President, he had no problem sacrificing everything for the club – even laying down his own life, time and time again, if it meant protecting his family. I respected him for that, and was honored to be a part of it. "I know what's really going on here. You can blame this on whatever you want, but the truth is glaring you right in the face."

"He's my son! What kind of man would I be if I put him in danger? I can't risk it, Cotton," I told him, as I looked down at my broken arm that was now wrapped up in a sling. I was a fucking mess. Bruises and cuts covered my body from head to toe. They'd done a pretty good job of working me over, and I still couldn't figure out why they didn't just kill me when they had the chance. "Think about it. What if he was with me when those motherfuckers jumped me? It's up to me to protect him, and I couldn't live with myself if something happened to him. I already ruined his mother's life, and I'll be damned if I ruin his."

"That's bullshit, and you know it. Hailey brought that shit on herself. You can't keep carrying all of the blame," Cotton snapped.

"It was my fault! All if it! I wasn't there when she needed me. I should have stuck with her, made sure she got the help she needed. Now she's dead, and I have to own that. John Warren is all I have left of her. I can't let anything happen to him."

"Nothing's going to happen to him, Maverick," he assured me, but we both knew he couldn't guarantee that. "None of that even matters… it's all in the past. Right now, you have to face your demons, either fight them or learn to live with them."

I knew he was right. My mind had been a cluster fuck since the day I brought John Warren home with me. When I looked at him, I could tell that he had my blood running through his veins. He was such a good looking kid – healthy and strong. I was thankful that his mother's drug use hadn't hurt him. Yet, there was a question lingering deep inside of me. I couldn't put my finger on it. Why did this strange pull keep going off in my head? I loved this kid from the start, but my mind was bombarded with doubts – some of which I couldn't even name. I had to believe that I was doing this for him. I'd fucked up so much already, I couldn't be responsible for ruining another life. Me… the club… whatever the reason, John Warren didn't belong here with me. He deserved more.

"I can't take that chance. I can't make the same mistakes again, Cotton." My throat tightened, making it difficult to even say the words. I truly believed that taking him to Lily was the right thing to do. He deserved a mother, and I knew she loved him as her own. But, the selfish side of me wished things could be different. Still, I knew I had to protect him at all costs. That was the most important thing now.

"Maverick…" Cotton tried again.

"I need you to back me up on this," I argued. "It's the right thing for John Warren… and for me."

His face was registered with acceptance as he brought his hand up, and rested it on my shoulder. "I wish you'd give it more time, but if this is what you think you should do, I'll support you on it. When do you need to leave?"

I stood up and reached for my keys. "Tonight. There's no need in delaying this thing any longer. It's a long drive, so it will take me a couple of days to get back."

"I'll let the guys know. Just be careful," Cotton told me as I turned towards the door. "Maverick?"

I looked over towards him as Cotton said, "Some choices can't be undone. You need to be sure about this one, brother." My eyes dropped down to the floor. The worn out boards creaked beneath my feet, and I wondered how they managed to support my weight. I felt so heavy, like the unrelenting weight of the world was pressing down on my shoulders. It hurt to move... to even breathe. His words circled through my thoughts, and I knew he was right. This one decision could haunt me for the rest of my life, but I knew in my gut it was the right thing to do for John Warren... for my son.

I opened the door to my room, and stopped. It was hard to believe how much this room had changed in just one week. It'd been just a room. A place to crash when I needed it, but now I didn't recognize it. John Warren's presence filled the air, surrounding me with his warmth. My chest tightened as I thought about him not being here anymore. I tried to block the turmoil from my mind as I grabbed a bag and quickly began filling it with his clothes and toys. When I picked up the tiny giraffe that he slept with every night, I couldn't hold it together any longer. My legs began to buckle under me when I thought about him lying in that crib with his tiny little fingers wrapped around the giraffe's neck. It gutted me. I dropped down to my knees as I held the stuffed animal tightly in my hands, bringing it up close to my face so I could inhale JW's scent. Damn. I'd never felt a hurt like this before.

Why did it have to be like this? Why couldn't I be the father he needed? What the fuck was wrong with me? My chest tightened when I thought about taking him back to Lily. My heart shattered like broken glass when I thought about not being able to see his smile; to touch him… to hold him. He was a part of me – the best part of me – but I couldn't stop the doubts from spiraling through my head. The darkness inside of me was growing, engulfing me. John Warren deserved more than I could give… a life not tarnished by the likes of me.

There was a tap on my door, and I had just enough time to get back on my feet before Cassidy walked in. John Warren was propped up on her hip with a handful of her hair in one hand and a bottle in the other. "I just finished giving little man his dinner and a bath. He's all ready for bed."

"Thanks, Cass." She was one of the bartenders at the club. Even though she sometimes partied with the club girls, I trusted her to watch him. She'd come to love the kid in the short time he'd been here and enjoyed spending time with him. From the moment I brought him into the club, she couldn't get enough of him, always wanting to hold him and play with him. Cass adored him, and I honestly wouldn't have known what to do without her.

I rubbed my eyes with the palm of my hands, trying to clear the tears away. When she noticed the expression on my face, she asked, "What's going on? Are you ok?"

"Would you believe me if I said yes?" I responded, as I looked away from her and started to put the last of John Warren's things in his bag.

"Seriously," she snapped. "Tell me what's going on, Maverick? Are you taking him somewhere?"

I took a deep breath and swallowed hard, trying to reign in the emotions that threatened to tear me apart. I had to hold it together. "I'm taking him back to Lily and Goliath. They can give him what he needs… the life that he deserves…"

"What? No! You can't do that, Maverick… He belongs here, with us… with *you*. You're his dad. You're all he needs," Cassidy cried as the tears began to pool in her eyes.

"Look at him, Cassidy. He's perfect. So innocent… so pure. All the good in the world is wrapped up in him." She looked down at him, a grief-stricken expression on her beautiful face. "I'm no good for him. I'll only fuck it all up if I keep him here. I love him. I love him like nothing else, and I have to protect him… protect him from my world… protect him from *me*." I could feel the storm of emotions begin to take hold again, so I took JW from her arms and picked up his bag. "I don't expect you to understand it, Cassidy, but this is something I have to do. I have to do this for him."

"Please… please don't do this," she begged as she grabbed my arm. Her eyes pleaded with me to listen as she said, "This is a mistake. You're going to regret this for the rest of your life!" I couldn't listen to anymore. Trying my best to block out her cries, I walked past her and out the door.

I was relieved to see that the parking lot was empty as I sat John Warren into his car seat. When I clicked his seatbelt around him, he reached for my hand and smiled. That smile would be forever burned into my mind. I took his little hand and brought it up to my mouth, gently kissing the fingers that wrapped around mine. "I love you, JW. Always will."

I handed the little guy his giraffe as I put the rest of the bags in the seat beside him. I closed his door and got into the car. I sat there for a few minutes in the silence, trying to pull my shit together. Everything was so quiet. It was like I was stuck in some kind of nightmare, lost in a deep fog, and then JW started to babble. He was talking to me like I knew exactly what he was saying.

I turned back to him and said, "I know, little buddy. I know."

I wiped the tears from my eyes and started the engine. It didn't take him long to fall asleep, leaving me with a whirlwind of thoughts and questions. I still couldn't believe how much had happened over the past year. If I had just known... if I hadn't been so stupid and realized everything that was really going on with Hailey, maybe things could have been different.

I'll never forget the first time I laid eyes on her. I'd pulled my bike into an old diner out on Highway 19. It was an out of the way spot, but it was raining, and I was wet and cold. The moment I saw her walk across the floor, I wasn't cold anymore. She was waiting tables, and I wondered why a sexy woman like her was working at a place like this in the middle of nowhere. She had a figure that made a man want to peel her clothes right off, and I would've done just about anything to do just that. I instantly craved the touch of her skin against mine. Fuck... my whole body tensed and my dick jumped up in need every time she even passed by me. Her long black hair was pulled back into a ponytail show-ing off the most beautiful blue eyes I'd ever seen. Her smile though, that mouth, those lips… damn, she was *perfect*.

One date was all it took. After that, the months rolled by so fast that I lost track of time. It was a whirlwind. She was everything I ever thought I wanted and more. She liked being on the back of my bike and enjoyed hanging with my brothers at the clubhouse. We spent hours talking and drinking with them. She fit. I loved that. We were happy. We'd even started talking about our future, making plans for our life to-gether. She had enrolled in a nursing program and worked every day at the diner to pay for her tuition. Life was good.

Then the nightmare hit. Everything went up in smoke. It was hell. A stupid drunk crashed into Hailey's car, leaving her severely wounded. The dashboard crushed in on her, breaking her leg and fracturing several vertebrae in her neck. It was my fault. I was being selfish that night. I just wanted to be with her every second, and I didn't listen when she told me she was too tired to come to the club. She'd been working all day and just wanted to go home. I should have listened to her, but I was too selfish. I'd had a long day and just wanted inside her.

That crash stole her spark and replaced it with pain and anguish. Her injuries were so painful that the doctors prescribed her strong pain medication, and it seemed to help, giving her some relief from her misery. After she'd been home for a while, I noticed that she was taking too many pills. I figured she was just hurting, and since she was going to school to be a nurse, I thought that she knew what she was doing. A month later, when I saw her taking three at a time, I confronted her about it. She became defensive, but finally admitted that she might have a problem. As time went on, I tried to get her help, sending her to rehab and trying to find doctors that could stop the pain. But nothing worked. The pull of her addiction was already too strong. She tried to hide it from me, over and over again. Each time I discovered that she was still using, she'd promise to try harder. She'd swear that she loved me, and would do whatever it took to get better. I believed her, until the day I found *another* hidden stash of pills. That day, I knew I was done. She chose the drugs over the life we shared, and I refused to be a part of it.

The day I walked out of her life, I prayed that she would straighten herself out and find her way back to me. Instead, she became more and more determined to get her hands on her next fix. When her desperation took hold, she decided to give information about our club in exchange for more drugs. Her betrayal to the club was a deci-sion we'd both come to regret. I should have known that if she would do something like that, she was way past just being in trouble… her life was in true jeopardy. I should've seen she was still struggling, and tried harder to help her. But in truth, it was too late… her lies would send her to her grave. All of her damn lies.

She disappeared for months. No one knew where she was. The club never lets a betrayal go. They searched for her and finally found out that she had been living in a small town just outside of Washington. It looked like she was finally getting her shit together. She'd gotten a job and had a nice place to live. She'd even had a baby. Her neighbor said Hailey was really trying, but it all fell apart. It was just too much for her, and she ended up taking the baby to her mother. My brothers found her dead in her apartment from a drug overdose. It was obvious that it was no accident. Her death hit me hard. I couldn't help but blame myself for what had happened, and the guilt of her death was crippling. But it was nothing compared to the hurt that I felt when I discovered the mountain of secrets she had kept hidden from me.

It was several months after her death when I got an unexpected phone call from a hospital in Paris, Tennessee. A nurse called to tell me that my son had just been in an accident. *My* son. I felt like someone had knocked the wind out of me when I heard those words. My name was listed on his birth certificate, right under Hailey's. It was right there in black and white. I never dreamed the kid that she'd had was mine, and now I had missed almost a year of his life, because Hailey never told me about him. Instead, she took our son to her mother, asking her to protect him from me. Trying to keep her promise, Hailey's mother sent John Warren away. She decided that Lily was the only one that could keep him safe from me and my club. Lily packed him up, and took off for Tennessee. I would have never even known about my son if it hadn't been for his accident. Her mother prayed that I would never find out. She blamed me for Hailey's death. In truth, she was right. Hailey would still be alive if she hadn't been with me. I will never forgive myself for what happened. I had failed her then, but I wouldn't fail her again. I wouldn't let anything happen to our son. I would make sure that he had the life that I couldn't give his mother.

I could barely keep my eyes open by the time I pulled into Lily's driveway. It was Christmas Eve, and the house was lit up with lights, making what I was about to do feel even more impossible. I tried to shake it off. This wasn't about me. It was about John Warren. Giving him a life like this… filled with Christmas trees and family. The life I'd never be able to give him.

Goliath lived the club life, and although his

club was different, *safer*, he understood the danger that came along with it. He would know better than anyone why I had to do this. As VP of the Devil Chaser's, he'd seen the hard times of living in a one percenters' club… the uncertainty… the danger. They had put that all behind them, and his club had worked hard to become a legitimate club that was focused on the brotherhood and their families. It was one of the things that I respected most about these men. Nothing was more important than keeping their families safe. I put the car in park, and by the time I turned off the engine and opened the car door, Lily was standing on the front porch.

"What happened to you? Are you ok?" she asked. Her eyes filled with fright as she studied my cuts and bruises. I knew I looked like hell, but I had no intention of telling her what had happened. When I didn't answer, she asked, "What are you doing here, Maverick?"

"I need to talk to you and Goliath. Is he here?" I asked her. I knew I was the last person she expected to see tonight, and I hated that I had scared her.

"I just got off the phone with him. He said he'd be here in 5 minutes. Come on in, and we'll wait for him inside," she told me as she turned towards the front porch.

"Give me a second. John Warren is still sleeping in the car. Let me get him," I said as I reached for the car door.

"John Warren? He's here with you? Is he okay?" Her voice was high pitched, almost breaking into a cry as she spoke. Her eyes widened with dismay as she watched me pull John Warren out of his car seat. The second I got him out, she raced over to me and took him from my arms. I instantly felt the loss of his touch, and fought the urge to take him back from her. The look on his face stopped me. His eyes lit up with excitement as he reached out to her, making me realize just how much he loved her… he was where he belonged.

"He's here. I can't believe he's really here!" she cried, tears streaming down her face.

John Warren looked up at her and smiled. He reached for the collar of her shirt and squealed. Lily's eyes danced with excitement as she looked at him. I took a deep breath, and began to feel a sense of relief. Lily loved him. There was no doubt in my mind that she would care for him like she was his own mother.

"I don't understand. You have to tell me what's going on, Maverick," she pleaded.

"Let's go inside and wait for Goliath."

I reached into the backseat and grabbed John Warren's bags, and Lily followed me through the front door. She cautiously watched as I set his bags on the floor. We were just sitting down on the sofa when I heard Goliath's bike pull into the driveway. Lily jumped up and met him at the front door.

"Goliath…." she said stopping him at the front door. He looked down at John Warren in Lily's arms, searching for any sign that something might be wrong. He finally looked over to me, noticing my broken arm and all the bruises that marked my body.

"Maverick, what the hell is going on?" Goliath asked as he stepped inside.

"I really don't know where to start."

"Start with what happened to you," Lily said as she walked over to the sofa and sat down beside me. "Are you okay?"

"Yeah… it's nothing. I trusted the wrong person, and it cost me," I said as I looked down to the floor, unable to look at her. The irony of it being her sister that I'd trusted was too much for me to bare.

"You gonna tell us why you're here?" Goliath asked.

I laid my head in my hands, trying to search for the right words to say. After a few seconds of silence, I drug my fingers through my hair, trying to calm my nerves. I looked over to Lily and said, "I just can't do it to him. I love him, Lily. I really do. I love him enough to know that he needs more than I can give him right now." Overwhelmed with all the mixed emotions churning inside me, I stood up. My heart was racing, and I began pacing back and forth. I needed to make them understand. They needed to know why I had to do this. "I let Hailey down. I should've done more. Should've protected her, but I fucked up. I don't deserve to have JW. I'll just fuck it up."

"You're being too hard on yourself, Maverick. Hailey made those choices. Not you. No one blames you," Lily told me, trying to calm me down.

"*I do*," I stopped pacing, and looked directly at her. "I should've been there for Hailey. Instead, she sank into the darkness where no one could save her. I can't let that happen to JW."

"I don't understand. What exactly are you saying?" she asked me.

"I came here to see… to ask if…" I swallowed my pride and my own broken heart and said, "I wanted to know if you and Goliath would take John Warren… raise him as your own. I want to be everything he needs, but I know I'm not. I can't give him what you can."

"But why now?" Lily asked, as she looked down at my son, her hand softly brushing over the top of his head.

"Lots of reasons. More than I care to explain. Let's just say a baby doesn't exactly fit in the life I'm living right now." The thoughts of them beating me with that crow bar flashed through my mind, and I winced in remembrance of the pain they inflicted. It didn't come close to the agony I was feeling at this moment, but it reassured me that I was making the right choice for him.

"Are you sure about this Maverick? You have to know that I want him, but I need you to be sure. I couldn't take losing him again," Lily said.

"He means the world to me. He's the one truly good thing I've done with my life. I hate the thought of losing him, but I just can't do this to him. He deserves more."

"Maverick, we'll want to adopt him if he stays with us. You gonna be okay with that?" Goliath asked. Lily looked over to him with surprise, and I could see the love and wonder in her eyes when she looked at him. A small smile spread across her face when she realized what he was saying. Now, I knew Goliath wanted him just as much as she did.

"I get that. Yeah, I'd be okay with that, but I still want to see him. I want him to know who I am, so that one day, when he's older, he'll understand why I did this," I explained. I knew it was a lot to ask, but I couldn't imagine never seeing him again. I needed to know that I could still have some kind of contact with him, or I wouldn't be able to survive this.

"You will always be welcome here, Maverick. I want John Warren to know you, too. It takes a special kind of person to love someone enough to let them go," Lily told me with tears in her eyes.

"I wish I could be more for him. I wish I could be the father that he needs, but I know you both love him. You'll give him the kind of life I can't."

"We'll do our best. I can promise you that," Goliath said confidently.

"Thank you for trusting us with him. We'll do everything we can to make him happy," Lily promised. JW reached out his hands for Goliath. He walked over and took him from Lily's arms. He rested his head against Goliath's chest like he was meant to be there. Goliath ran his hand over his little head and down his back as he hugged him closer.

Goliath kissed JW on the head and said, "Glad you're back Little Man. We've missed you."

I couldn't take it any longer. One more second of this, and I was going to fall apart. "I'm going to head back."

"You can stay here tonight," Lily offered.

"Thanks Lily, but I need to get back. We've got some shit going down back home, and my president needs me to get back. I'll be in touch."

"Okay, but you are more than welcome. The door is always open. Just let us know when you want to come back for a visit."

"I'll be back. You can count on that. If you

ever need me, I'm just a phone call away. Thank you both. I know in my gut that this is the right thing to do." I walked over to JW and kissed him on the side of his head. I laid my hand on his back and stared at him for a minute. I leaned over and whispered in his ear, "Don't hate me for this. I wouldn't do it if it wasn't the right thing to do. I *love* you." I couldn't stop the tears from filling my eyes as I walked out to my car.

Chapter 2

HENLEY

Six Months Later

"ARE YOU REALLY going to keep your face buried in that book all night?" Cassidy asked.

"You know, I have my final tomorrow. I need to make an A in this class," I told her without looking up from my book.

"You have to make an *A* in every class. It's like you've forgotten how to have fun. I miss *fun* Henley. What happened to her?" she said as she looked in the mirror and played with her hair. "You need to go out with some friends and have a good time."

"Yadda, yadda, yadda… I'll go out and celebrate when I finish my finals."

"Why don't you come to the club with me tonight? The guys are having a party, and I know they'd love to see you. I miss hanging out with you. Let's go out and have some fun like we used to."

"Ummm… how about *NO*?" I answered sarcastically.

I had nothing against going to the clubhouse with Cassidy. I actually kind of liked going there from time to time. The guys were a little rough around the edges, but they all seemed like pretty decent guys. It didn't go unnoticed however, that they all liked Cassidy… *a lot*. The way they pawed all over her, made me feel a little uncomfortable sometimes. But I've done my best to avoid asking her questions about it. She's not one to talk about what really goes on at the club. Besides, I learned a long time ago that Cassidy has a mind of her own, and it's best to just leave her to it. She was happy—that was all that mattered. The Satan's Fury MC had become like a second family to her, and I knew she loved them… all of them. I'll admit that I've even found myself a little jealous of the life she has created outside of ours, but I'd never tell her that.

"Oh… come on. Don't be a 'Debbie Downer'. It'll be fun. We can have a few drinks and dance on my break…," she encouraged as she shook her hips from side to side. The bangles on her wrist clanked together as she tugged at the hem of her mini skirt. As she looked in the mirror, Cassidy pulled her hair up in a messy bun, and touched up her make-up. She was club ready. I smiled to myself thinking how different she looked an hour ago when she was sprawled out in front of the TV eating potato chips and chocolate chip cookies in her pajamas. Her transformation was complete.

"Maybe some other time," I told her as I flipped through the pages of my textbook. "I'm just not up to partying tonight. Besides, you know I've got to get up early in the morning."

"Okay, then let's do something else then. We could go grab a burger and watch a movie? I'll get one of the girls to cover my shift. You know I hate leaving you here all alone, Lee Bug."

"I'm fine, Cass. I really do need to study. I'll go with you next time… promise. Go have a good time. I'll be here when you get back."

"Ok. Have it your way, but you know you've got this. You've been studying for weeks," she said as she reached for her purse. "You know where to find me if you need me."

"Try to behave," I told her playfully.

"Always," she said giving me a wink.

I watched her walk out the door. Silence quickly filled the apartment as soon the door closed behind her. Questioning my choice to stay home, I took a deep breath and tried to focus on my notes. Studying right now was pointless; it was just too freaking quiet. Every little noise became a distraction, and I couldn't concentrate. Deciding it was time for a break, I reached for the remote and started scrolling through all the endless channels of sitcoms and infomercials. I finally stopped on some detective show that my dad always liked to watch. I couldn't help but feel a little homesick when I saw his favorite character appear on the screen, so I grabbed my phone and called him.

He picked up on the first ring, "Hey there, sweetheart. How's it going?" Just hearing his voice brought a big smile to my face.

"Hey, daddy. Everything's great. I have my last final tomorrow, and then I have some time off before the summer semester starts."

"Why don't you just take the summer off? Take Cassidy and go to the beach for a few days… or come home for a visit. You know I'd love to see you." I felt a twinge of guilt when I thought about him being there all alone. Even though it'd been several years since mom left, he was still having a hard time adjusting to not having her there.

"You know I'd love that, but I've got a lot going on. I'll see what I can work out," I told him.

"You need to get out and see the world. You're only young once, you know."

"I'll see plenty once I graduate. Promise," I answered. "You worry too much."

"That's what fathers do. What about your sister? What's she up to these days?" he asked apprehensively. Dad wasn't exactly happy about her working as a bartender at an MC's clubhouse, but he'd given up trying to talk to her about it. Actually, they barely talk at all anymore, and I can tell it bothers him.

"She's doing great. Just left for work a few minutes ago."

"Ok… well, keep an eye on her. You know I worry," he said softly.

"I will, daddy. She's happy… really." I waited a few seconds for him to say something, but he remained quiet. Finally, I said, "Well… I guess I better get back to studying."

"Ok, sweetheart. Call me later and let me know how you did on your exams. And, think about what I said. It would do you some good to take the summer off. You've worked really hard. You deserve to go out and have some fun."

"Ok. I'll think about it. Talk to you soon," I told him as I hung up the phone.

I tried to get back to studying, but searching through the endless pages of notes was making me stir crazy, and my growling stomach was making it hard to focus. I hadn't stopped study-ing long enough to eat dinner, and it was finally catching up with me. I grabbed the bag of chips that Cassidy left on the coffee table, and when I put my hand in the bag, I only found a mound of crumbs. I tossed the bag into the garbage and went to the kitchen to search for something to eat. We were down to milk, eggs, and an old veggie tray. That wasn't going to work. It was time to make a snack run.

Chapter 3

MAVERICK

WITH A TWIST of my wrist, I throttled the accelerator and the sound of the engine roared to life around me. The wind whipped against my face as I sped down the long, curvy road to nowhere. Nothing helped me clear my head like the feel of the raw power radiating from the machine beneath me. The wind. The open road. The freedom. It's just a matter of time, but I knew that it was out there waiting for me. *Peace*.

I'd gotten to know this highway pretty well over the past few months. He'd never admit it, but I knew these runs were Cotton's way of keeping me busy. He knew it's what I needed right now. Giving up John Warren had almost broken me, and focusing all of my attention on the club was helping me reconcile with some of my demons. Today, he sent me to meet up with Nitro to handle the payment for this month's shipment. He was waiting for me in the upstairs loft of an old warehouse. Each time we met, it was somewhere different… a bar, an apartment, or the back of an SUV. Nitro always made sure he covered his tracks, and Cotton trusted him. He was the only one that we dealt with when it came to the gun trafficking side of our club. He was older and had been around the block long enough to know a good deal when he saw it.

"You again? I'm beginning to think that you like coming to see me," he said with a smirk, his dark eyes peering at me. His sarcasm didn't go unnoticed, but I decided to ignore it. I learned a long time ago that Nitro was a smart ass, and it was best to keep things short. The last thing I needed was to mingle words with him today.

"Cotton wants the shipment doubled for next month. Is that going to be a problem?" I asked.

"Nope. Not a problem at all. I'll take care of it," he answered as he wrote himself a note and then shoved it into the back pocket of his jeans.

"I'll let him know," I said as I handed him the thick envelope full of cash. "This should settle us up for now."

"Right on, brother. I'm sure I'll be seeing you soon."

I gave him a quick nod and headed back for my bike. As the miles back home blurred into one another, I found myself thinking about my younger brother, Gavin. I had been thinking about him a lot lately. It just hasn't been the same since the day he left for Tennessee. I couldn't stop thinking about the conversation we'd had about him leaving. It was a talk that I hadn't been looking forward to having, but I knew it was inevitable. It was something we'd discussed several times over the past year. Gavin was bound and determined to follow my footsteps into the club life. It was getting harder and harder to put him off. Gavin is a good kid, and any club would be lucky to have him. But if he truly wanted to prospect for Satan's Fury, he would have to wait until things settled down at the club. He'd need to have time to adjust before all hell broke loose, and rest assured – all hell would break loose.

When I pulled up in his driveway that day, he was in his workshop. As usual, he was covered in grease while he worked on his bike. Restoring old Harleys was his passion, and he'd spent every free minute he had out in his garage. For a twenty year old, he had a talent like no one I had ever known. He could take a piece of junk and turn it into a work of art in a matter of a few days.

"I was beginning to think you were going to blow me off again," Gavin whispered under his breath, as he continued to disassemble the engine.

"Told you I'd be here. I had some things to take care of first."

"Yeah…well, I've heard that before," he grunted.

"You going to tell me what you wanted to talk about?" I asked as I walked over to the mini-refrigerator and got us both a beer. I twisted off the tops and placed one on the table next to him.

"Been thinking about a few things," he said.

"This ought to be good," I grumbled under my breath.

"Why do you do that? You know what… just forget it. I don't need this shit from you right now. Just go," he barked as he motioned towards the door.

"Just tell me what the hell you've been thinking about, Gavin." I grabbed a wrench and started helping him remove the different screws that were corroded with rust and grime from the old engine.

He glared at me for a few seconds before he finally said, "I want to move to Tennessee."

"What the hell are you talking about?" He'd caught me off guard. That was the last thing I expected to hear from him right now.

"I want to go prospect for the Devil Chasers."

"Gavin," I barked.

"Just hear me out before you fly off the handle. You told me that you didn't want me prospecting for your club right now because of all the shit that's going on. I get that, but I've heard you talk about Goliath and his club. You've said yourself that you liked being there. I've always wanted to have a place where I could work on bikes, and they're known all over the country for the restorations they do. Prospecting for them makes sense," he said sounding hopeful. "Besides, if I prospected at your club, I'd always be following under your shadow. I want a chance to make a name for myself... without all the bullshit."

"It wouldn't be like that, Gavin."

"It would, and you know it. You've already made your mark on the club. I want to be able to do the same. Besides, being in Tennessee would also give me a chance to keep an eye on John Warren."

"What makes you think they'll even take you on? They don't know a damn thing about you."

"I was hoping that you'd talk to Goliath. Put in a good word for me."

Fuck. I couldn't believe what he was asking. The very thought of him prospecting for another club was difficult to digest, but one so far away made it impossible to comprehend. How the hell was I supposed help him leave? Deep down, I knew it was the perfect place for him to prospect, but the thought of losing him – my brother, the only link to my life before the club, was hard for me to accept. "You have to give me some time to think about this."

"Fuck, Maverick! You need to stop thinking so damn much. Since we lost Hailey, you've been ..." he started.

"We? What the fuck are you talking about?" I shouted, stepping closer to him. "We didn't lose Hailey. I'm the one that loved her, and I'm the one that lost her. Hell, I'm the one that got fucked over by all of her damn lies!"

"You weren't the only one who lost her, Maverick. You know I cared for her, too. More than you know." His eyes flickered with a hurt that I didn't quite understand.

"What are you trying to say here, Gavin?"

"I'm saying get your head out of your ass and realize that you weren't the only one that got hurt by everything that happened with Hailey. It was hard on all of us to lose her, but it's time to move on. You're twenty-six years old, but you're acting like your life is over," he explained as he dropped his tools on the table. *"It's time for both of us to move on. Moving to Tennessee ..."*

"I said I'd think about it, Gavin. That's all I'm willing to give you right now."

We spent the next few hours working in the garage in silence. I thought about everything he said, and I honestly couldn't find a reason for him not to go. Working with the Devil Chasers would be a great opportunity for him, and I knew they'd take care of him. I hated that it really was the best option for him. I wasn't ready to let him go, but I couldn't hold him back.

Once we'd finished disassembling the engine, I turned to him and said, "I'll call Goliath in the morning and see what he thinks about you coming down."

"Thanks, Maverick. I'll do my best to make you proud..."

"Gavin, I can't remember a time when I wasn't proud of you."

I've talked to him several times since the day

he packed his bags and left. He truly seemed happy. As hard as it was to admit, he was right. He was already making a name for himself in their garage, and I was proud of him for taking the risk. That didn't mean I didn't miss him.

Chapter 4

HENLEY

WHEN I PULLED up at the convenience store, it was already almost midnight, and there were no other cars in the parking lot. Even with my shorts on, the heat of the night instantly brought a light sheen of sweat on my skin when I got out of my car. A chime rang out when I opened the store door, and the cashier briefly looked up from her magazine as she watched me walk inside. Once she'd acknowledged my presence with an unappreciative sneer, she looked back down at her magazine. When I reached into the refrigerator for my soda, the bite of the cold air from the freezer brought goosebumps to my skin. I quickly closed the door, and tried to shake off the chill by rubbing my hand up and down my arm.

I walked down each and every aisle looking for something decent to eat. When I couldn't make up my mind, I just started filling my arms anything and everything that looked like it might curb my growing hunger. By the time I made it up to the counter, my hands were loaded with an embarrassing amount of drinks, chips, and chocolate.

"Did you find everything you need?" the lady asked without ever really looking up at me. She obviously wasn't happy that I was interrupting her reading time.

"Yeah, I think so," I told her as I looked around the store, feeling slightly ashamed at the enormous amount of junk food sitting in front of me.

After an excruciating amount of time, she finally said, "That'll be $24.96."

I swiped my debit card, and when the receipt printed, I quickly grabbed my heavy bag of goodies and headed out into the empty parking lot. As I walked towards my car and started to open the door, I heard a loud thud coming from the side of the store. At first I ignored it, but then I heard it again… louder. I knew I should have just gotten in my car and left, but my curiosity got the best of me. I threw my bag in the front seat and crept quietly over to the dark side of the building. I knew dumb shit like this was what got people into trouble, but I honestly hoped there'd be nothing to it. I just kept thinking that the sales clerk must have decided to pull herself away from her magazine long enough to take out the trash. Little did I know, I was wrong… terribly wrong.

As soon as I made it to the edge of the building, there was another loud crash followed by the sounds of feet scuffling against the concrete. I couldn't see anything. It was just too damn dark. So I quietly stepped into the shadows, and waited for my eyes to adjust to the lack of light. Shit! Suddenly it wasn't just noise as the sounds of a man's grunts and anguished cries echoed along the wall of the building, making my heart nearly jump out of my chest. A feeling of terror washed over me as I realized someone was in trouble. I took one step closer, and my world instantly stopped moving. A man was standing with his back to me, and even though, I had no idea who he was, I instantly recognized his black vest with the dark red embroidery scrolled on the back. He was a member of the Satan's Fury MC, and something was wrong… very wrong.

I was turning to go for help when I heard, "We're done playing games with you asshole."

"Fuck you. I'm not telling you a goddamn thing."

"Then your time is up, *brother*." Two gunshots rang out and my heart stopped as I watched his head jerk back when the bullets slammed into his chest. As I watched his limp body drop to the ground, I felt like someone punched me in the stomach, knocking the wind out of me. I couldn't breathe… couldn't move. I was absolutely frozen with fear. I looked behind me, praying for someone to be there – a car driving by or someone walking down the street; anyone to help me escape this nightmare, but there was no one. The darkness of the night engulfed me as I realized that I was completely alone, except for these monsters standing just a few feet away from me that had just killed a member of the Satan's Fury club. The hairs on the back of my neck prickled against my skin as I listened to the dying man gasping for breath… then there was nothing, just deafening silence. He was lying dead just a few feet from me, and there was nothing I could do to help him. An overwhelming sense of panic surged through my body as I realized how bad this really was. A small whimper escaped my lips as my chest tightened, and my legs began to tremble beneath me.

I was about to completely lose it when I heard, "HEY!"

One of the men had spotted me; the sound of his voice startled me back to reality. Before I had time to think, a massive shadow began stalking towards me.

"I… uh… I… shit!" I screeched as I twirled around and raced towards my car. My legs felt like jelly as I ran, making me feel like I was moving in slow motion. Behind me, the sounds of boots hitting the pavement filled me with pure terror. I was freaking out. The footsteps were getting closer, and I just knew they were going to get me. I was going to die in the middle of a convenience store parking lot! I ran with everything I had and was relieved when I saw that my car door was still open. My entire body was shaking as I jumped inside and locked the doors. I started the engine, threw it in reverse, and stomped on the gas! I heard one of them hit the back of my car as I sped towards the main road. When I looked in my rear view mirror, two large men were standing under the light of the convenience store… staring at the back of my vehicle with pure rage in their eyes. They were after more blood… *mine.*

When they were finally out of sight, I reached down in my purse for my phone. I quickly dialed Cassidy's number.

"Come on… come on. Answer the damn phone," I shouted. After calling three times without an answer, I gave up. Everything that happened kept racing through my mind. I had to tell someone. Cassidy told me that the club didn't do cops, but I didn't know what else to do.

"This is 911. State your emergency," the operator calmly said.

My hands were shaking, and I was finding it difficult to speak. I took a deep breath and said, "I just witnessed a shooting behind the S&K

Quick Mart! There were these two guys, and they shot a man in the alley. I didn't know what to do and … and… those men… oh my god, I… I think they saw me! They were…"

"Miss, I need you to try to calm down. I am sending an officer to that location now. I will need your name and a phone number where you can be reached," she answered.

"My name is Henley Gray." I stammered. I could barely tell the operator my phone number, my hands were shaking so badly that I could hardly hold on to the phone.

"Ma'am, as soon as the officers check the location of the shooting, they will call you to make a report. It shouldn't take long. Please stay close to your phone. I'm sure they will want to talk to you."

"Okay. I will. Thank you," I told her.

As soon as I got home, I searched the house for Cassidy. When she wasn't there, I tried calling her again. This time I left her a message, "Cassidy, I need you to call me. I saw something tonight. It was bad, and…" Without finishing, I hung up the phone. Those men had no idea who I was, and there was no reason for me to get all freaked out about it. I'd tell Cassidy what I saw when she got home and that would be the end of it. The club would take care of it.

I checked all the locks on the doors before curling up on the sofa, praying that my nerves would settle down, but being in this empty apartment wasn't making it easy. My test was first thing in the morning, and I desperately needed to get some sleep. I was finally about to drift off when my telephone rang.

"Hello?" I answered.

"Henley Gray?" a deep, raspy voice asked.

"Yes?"

"This is Officer Ronnie Donaldson, from the Williamson County Police Department. I'm calling about the report you made of a shooting at the S&K on Park Street."

"Yes, that was me. Did you catch them?"

"Ms. Gray, did you know that placing a false report is against the law," he scolded with his voice deep and forceful.

"What? What are you talking about?" I asked defensively.

"We went to the location, and there was no sign of any disturbance. It's the middle of the night, Ms. Gray. You wasted our time and the tax payers' dollars."

"That can't be right. I saw them…. They shot him right in front of me! There had to be something… a body or blood?" I pleaded with him, trying to make him believe me.

"There was nothing. I don't know what to tell you, Ms. Gray. We didn't find anything. If there really was a shooting, they did one hell of a job of covering their tracks."

"What am I supposed to do now?" I asked.

"We'll go back and check things out again in the morning. I'll contact you if we find anything," he said flatly. From the sound of his voice, I could tell that he had no intention of going back. I was regretting calling them in the first place. Hopefully, the club would be able to figure out what the hell happened.

Chapter 5

MAVERICK

M Y PHONE HAD been ringing for several minutes, before I managed to pull off the road to answer it. When I looked at the screen and saw that it was Guardrail, I immediately became uneasy. He wouldn't be calling so early in the morning unless there was something wrong. When he told me that Cotton had called us all in to meet at church, I knew without a doubt that something was off. It was in his voice… he sounded shaken, and it wasn't like him at all. Guardrail had been VP of Satan's Fury for as long as I could remember, and it took a lot to rattle him. Whatever was going on, it wasn't good.

When I drove through the gate, I was instantly overcome with a feeling of dread. The parking lot was filled with my brother's bikes, but everything was still. No music from the bar, no talking or laughing… just an eerie silence that sent chills down my spine. As soon as I parked my bike, I headed straight for the meeting room. All of the brothers were sitting around the long oak table, their faces marked with grief. There were no words or expressions of greetings – this was not a typical call to church.

"Have a seat, Maverick," Cotton ordered with a strained voice. "Been waiting on you to get started."

As soon as I took my seat, I looked over to Guardrail, searching for some sign of what the hell was going on. His face was completely void of expression as he looked at the wall in front of him. Yeah, something was definitely wrong. My eyes wandered over to Stitch. His face was twisted with anguish, and the veins around his neck pulsed with rage. I could feel the anger vibrating off of him as he sat back in his chair with his fists clenched tight. He was the club Enforcer, and at 6'9", he was not a man you wanted to tangle with. The hell that man was capable of inflicting would humble anyone. He'd never backed down from anything, and he had the scars to prove it, leaving no doubt how he got his road name. Looking at him, I could see the fury literally rolling off of him. Whoever had fucked up, Stitch was going to make them pay.

The tension in the room crackled around us as Cotton said, "As some of you already know, we lost one of our own last night."

Stitch slammed his fist down on the table as he growled, "Someone was trying to send us a message with Skidrow's death. Whoever the hell it was, they can consider the message fucking received!"

"There's no doubt that they were trying to make a statement. One of the prospects found him this morning out by the main gate... tossed out like trash by the side of the road," Cotton continued. Anger flashed through his eyes as he proceeded to explain everything that had happened. "His patch had been removed, and any sign of Satan's Fury on his body had been burned."

"Who do you think did this?" I asked, still trying to make sense of everything he'd just said. They hadn't just killed one of our brothers... they had insulted our club to the highest degree by desecrating any and all signs of our club's name on Skidrow's body.

"Tony's old crew wouldn't have the balls to do something like this. It had to be someone else," Guardrail scowled, as he looked over to me.

"I want every man on this. I want to know where he was... who he's been talking to. Hell, I want to know what he had for dinner last night. Any fucking thing that might help us find out who did this."

Everyone nodded in agreement. It would only be a matter of time before we were able to track down the motherfuckers that did this. Our club had eyes and ears in places no one would ever expect. Whoever had done this had fucked with the wrong club.

"All of you know that Maverick has more than proven himself as an invaluable asset to the club over the past few years. He'd give his life for anyone of you, and I'm naming him as Sergeant of Arms. Everyone in agreement say, Aye," Cotton motioned. Before I had time to protest, the room filled with chants of approval. Fuck.

"Done. Maverick, get with Big Mike. See what you two can find out and get back to me within the hour." Mike was the best hacker in the club, and if there was anything that might help us, he'd be the one to find it.

"You got it," I answered.

"Guardrail, we need to make arrangements for Skidrow. Make sure he gets the respect he deserves. Get Dallas to the clubhouse. I want eyes on her at all times," Cotton ordered as he stood up. Dallas was Skidrow's old lady, and we all knew she was going to take this hard. "Meeting adjourned."

It took several seconds for everyone to start moving. The shock of everything that had happened was still lingering in the room. Skid was one of those brothers that we all felt close to. He was always there when you needed him, and I was humbled that they thought I was the right man to follow in his footsteps.

Guardrail walked over to me and placed his hand on my shoulder. "You were the best choice. You and I both know that."

"It doesn't seem right. We haven't even put the man in the ground, and now we've replaced him... with *me,* no less."

"Now's the time. Do him proud, brother. He'd want this for you, too."

Chapter 6

HENLEY

M Y EYES BURNED as I answered the last question on my final. I couldn't sleep at all last night, and my body literally ached from exhaustion. After turning in my exam, I headed out of the building towards my car. I was distracted as I searched for my keys that had gotten lost in the bottomless pit of my purse, therefore I almost didn't see the two men who were leaning against my car. They were having a heated conversation and were totally unaware that I was even coming in their direction. I had no idea who they were, but there was no doubt that they were there waiting for me. Trying not to call attention to myself, I slowly turned back towards the front door of the building. Once I was back inside, I looked out the window praying that they didn't see me. They were still talking when I grabbed my phone and called Cassidy.

"I was just about to call you. How was the final? Did you make your *A*?" she asked.

"I've been trying to call you all night, Cassidy. Why didn't you answer your damn phone?" I shouted.

"I'm sorry, Lee Bug. I didn't even hear my phone ringing. You know how loud it is when these guys have a party," she apologized.

"I think I'm in trouble, Cassidy. *Bad trouble*," I told her as my voice shook in fear.

"What do you mean? What's going on?"

"These two guys … they shot one of the men from your club, and I … I saw it. I saw it all, Cassidy. I tried to call you and tell you, but you didn't answer… and now… Oh shit! They're here! At my school… waiting out there by my car. What the hell am I supposed to do, Cassidy?"

"Skidrow," she mumbled.

"What?"

"Where are you right now?" she snapped.

"In one of the Biology labs."

"Okay… stay put. I'm sending someone to get you," she ordered. "What's the room number?"

"Mr. Yates' class. Room 132."

"It's going to be okay. Don't move from that spot," she assured me just before she hung up the phone.

After locking the door, I slumped down the wall and my butt hit the cold, hard floor with a thump. I felt so alone as I sat there thinking about how stupid I'd been. I had just gotten myself into one hell of a mess, and I only had myself to blame. I should've just gotten in my car and followed my initial instincts. I knew better. Nothing good ever comes from poking around in the dark.

I was still sitting on the floor when the sound of footsteps approached the door. Just as I was about to have a full blown panic attack, a man with a deep, raspy voice called out my name.

"Henley? Are you in there?" he called as he turned the handle of the locked door.

I was too afraid to speak. I had no idea who it was. By now whoever was after me had to know my name, and I couldn't be sure it wasn't them.

"Henley, it's me… Clutch. Cassidy sent us to find you. I need you to open the door," he said in a low whispering voice.

I quickly got up off the floor and unlocked the door. When I opened it, four members of the club were standing there staring at me. I instantly recognized Clutch and Scooter, but had no idea who the other two guys were. It didn't really matter… they were here to get me out of this mess, and I was grateful that they'd come. "Sorry, I wasn't sure who it was," I whispered.

"You did good, Henley. Are you okay?" Clutch asked. I didn't know him very well, but

Cassidy once told me that he was the club's Road Captain, whatever the hell that was. I didn't care about his title. I was just glad he was there.

"I'm fine. A little rattled, but I don't think they saw me," I answered as I fumbled with my purse. He stepped through the door, his large body towering over me and rested his hand on my shoulder. It was a small gesture, but his touch instantly calmed me. When I looked up at him, his fierce blue eyes were filled with concern. His face was hidden behind a long thick beard, making me wonder what was hidden beneath it. His eyes never left mine as he helped me gather up my things. There was something about the way he was looking at me that tugged at my heart. I couldn't stop staring at him. This man barely knew me, but he was willing to put himself in danger to help me. It wasn't just him – they were all here, putting their lives at risk for me.

Scooter cleared his throat, pulling me from my haze and said, "We checked the parking lot. The guys were gone, but they broke into your car." Scooter was one of the younger prospects, and was just too damn cute for his own good. He had one of those adorable baby faces, and all the tattoos in the world couldn't make him look like the tough guy he wanted to be. He was a good guy, and I'd always had fun hanging out with him when I went to the clubhouse with Cassidy.

"Did you have anything in your car that they

might have taken?" Clutch asked.

"Well, shit… my laptop. Was it still in there?" I asked hopefully.

"Nope. Looks like they got it, along with anything else you had in there," Scooter told me. "We'll do what we can to get it back."

"Shit… it has all my school stuff on it. Why would they need that?"

"They're going to do whatever they can to track you down, doll, but we're going to make sure that doesn't happen," Clutch said confidently. It freaked me out that those men had actually come after me, but it made me feel better knowing that the club would be there to protect me. "Let's get you back to the clubhouse. Cotton wants to talk to you."

"Cotton? Why do I suddenly feel like I'm being called to the principal's office?" When he didn't answer, a feeling of dread washed over me. The last thing I wanted to do was get the President of the Satan's Fury MC mad at me. I'd only met him a couple of times, but I knew he wasn't a man you wanted to get on your bad side. He was attractive, in an ominous sort of way. He was far from the oldest man in the club, but he was older than most. His white hair and goatee made him seem more distinguished, maybe a little superior to others. There was just something about him that made me feel… anxious. I'd always done my best to just be polite and avoid him as much as possible. He was the kind of man who commanded respect without saying a word, and now, I was going to have to actually talk to him – have a real conversation. What if I said the wrong thing? I didn't even know what to call him. President? President Cotton? President Cotton, sir? Oh hell, I was screwed.

All eyes were on me as I followed the four burly men down the hallway. They didn't fit the typical college scene with their leather vests and tattoos. I looked over at each of them, and realized how differently I saw them. These men may be rough, but they had shown me nothing but kindness. I knew they would do anything to protect me, and just walking with them, gave me a sense of security.

My rattled nerves slowly began to calm as we continued down the hallway. Several members of the football team scuttled out of the way as we walked past them. I watched as these tough football players unsuccessfully pretended that they weren't about to shit their pants as we passed by them. They were obviously threatened as they checked out the Satan's Fury patch on the back of Clutch's cut. The reaction from the females was vastly different. A couple of the hookers… I mean sluts… I mean *pretty girls,* smiled and flicked their long, beautiful hair as they tried their best to get the men's attention. My lips curved into a smile when their efforts were totally ignored. Yep... even though these men were here to save me from god-knows-what, I was walking down the hall smiling like a big dork.

With people still gawking at us, I followed Scooter over to his bike. After he helped me get my helmet on, I climbed on the back and rested my hands on his waist. The engine suddenly roared to life as Scooter throttled the ignition, and drove out the parking lot. The seat vibrated wildly beneath me as we picked up speed, quickly jetting into traffic. Surrounded by the others, we sped out onto the open highway towards the clubhouse. I'd never ridden on a bike before, and I loved it. As I held tightly onto Scooter, a feeling of pure ecstasy washed over me as we glided down the highway. The freedom... the bliss of being out on the open road thrilled me. The sound and speed was overwhelming, but I felt safe riding with Scooter. These guys rode with such confidence that it made them seem invincible. I was enjoying the ride so much, I almost forgot why I was with them. Once we pulled through the gate, reality came crashing down on me. As soon as they had parked their bikes, Clutch motioned for me to follow him through the back door.

"Cotton is in his office," he told me. My nerves jumped into overdrive when I took a step towards his office door, making it difficult to walk with my trembling knees.

"Okay," I answered wishing that he was going in, too. Dread washed over me as I tapped on the door. My heart jumped when he called out for me to come in. The door creaked loudly as I slowly opened his door.

"Hey… uh… President Cotton… sir? Clutch said you wanted to talk to me," I stammered.

He got up from his large wooden desk and walked over to me. Looking genuinely concerned he asked, "Are you okay?"

His voice was low and gentle, and it instantly set me at ease. "Yes, sir. I'm fine," I answered.

"Just call me Cotton. Come on in and have a seat," he offered as he picked up his phone and stated, "She's here. Come down to my office."

Just as he was settling back down in his seat, Maverick walked in. Shit! Now I had to deal with the two most intimidating men I'd ever met. I'll admit it, Maverick was good looking – extremely good looking, but damn, the man was a giant. As he made his way over to me, my eyes roamed over his large muscles that bulged beneath his tight black t-shirt. The scowl on his face was hard to ignore as he stood there glaring at me. Just being this close to him made me feel like I was twelve again. Without saying a word, he sat down next to me and waited for Cotton to speak.

"Henley, Cassidy told us that you saw something last night," Cotton said with a hopeful ring in his voice.

"I did. I tried to call her last night, but she couldn't hear her phone," I told him defensively.

"I need you to tell me everything you can remember. *Everything*," he demanded. The tiny crow's feet around his eyes crinkled as he spoke.

Without any interruptions, both men listened intently as I told them everything that had happened over the past twenty-four hours. I could see the anguish in their eyes as they listened to the details of their brother being shot. I tried my best not to leave anything out, but I was nervous, and it was hard to think straight.

"Did the cop ever call you back?" Maverick asked.

"No, but I could tell he was just trying to put me off," I explained as I clenched my hands together and rested them in my lap. "I'm pretty sure they thought I was lying. The guy said they found no evidence of a murder. I don't understand it. I mean… they shot him. He was bleeding. There had to be something."

"Guardrail and I went by earlier to check it out. There was no trace of blood anywhere. The place had been cleaned by someone who knew what he was doing," Maverick informed Cotton.

Cotton looked over to me and asked, "Can you tell us anything about these men you saw? Were they wearing cuts, or did any of them have tattoos?"

"They weren't wearing any leather, but one of them had a huge tattoo going down the length of his arm. I couldn't really make it out… a snake maybe? He had a long, dark beard and several piercings… a big dude, but not like you. He was just *fat.* The other one was tall and skinny and had his hair greased back. Kind of slimy looking. And, he had the same tattoo on his arm, along with another weird one on his cheek, just below his right eye. A tear or a star? I couldn't really tell. The guy talking had a slight accent. He didn't sound like he was from around here." My knees began to quiver involuntarily as I remembered how those men looked at me with rage in their eyes.

"Do you think you'd be able to recognize them if you saw them again?" Maverick questioned.

"I think so. They're pretty much burned into my memory."

"Were these the same men you saw by your car?" Cotton asked as he reached in his pocket for his cigarettes. His eyes never left mine as he brought one up to his mouth and lit it. He took a long drag, taking it deep into his lungs. The smoke slowly rolled through his lips as he exhaled, waiting for me to speak.

"No. Those guys were different, so it was probably nothing, just a coincidence," I explained. "I'm sure I just overreacted when I saw them at my car. I bet they were just after my laptop."

Maverick looked over to me and said, "There are no coincidences, Henley. Clutch found a tracking device hidden in the undercarriage of your car. It was there for a reason," he said firmly. Cold chills went down my spine as I thought about them hunting me down.

"We're going to keep you here for a while, so we can keep an eye on you. Make sure nothing happens to you," Maverick said.

"I really appreciate that, but I think I'll be fine. That's really not necessary. I'm sure that…" I started.

"It's not up for debate, Henley. As Sergeant of Arms, it's Maverick's job to protect the club and anyone tied to it. You are staying here, under his watch" Cotton demanded.

"Um… okay?" I agreed hesitantly. It was official. I was totally, utterly *screwed*.

Chapter 7

MAVERICK

"**H**OW DO YOU think it went? Do you think she has anything we can use?" Guardrail asked me.

"Yeah, but she was still pretty rattled. Hopefully, more will come to her later," I explained.

"You know she's under your watch until we get our hands on these motherfuckers. She's the only link we have to Skidrow's murder," he said, taking a drink from his beer.

The bar was quiet behind us. The news of Skid's death was hitting us all hard. It was always tough when we lost one of our own, but not knowing who killed Skid was only making it worse. His murder had blindsided us. The need for revenge filled the air, making us all on edge.

"I won't let anything happen to her," I assured him. As the new Sergeant of Arms, I knew her safety would fall to my hands. That didn't mean I was happy about it.

"That's all I needed to hear," he said as he stood up. "I need to go see about Dallas."

Just hearing Dallas's name made my chest tighten. The news of Skidrow's murder had just about broken her. They'd been together for as long as I could remember, and everyone knew they had something special. Skid was crazy about Dallas. Hell, he couldn't keep his damn hands off of her. He was always holding her and kissing her, every chance he got. He spent his life showing her what she meant to him, and he never once thought about straying. When their son Dusty was born with Down's syndrome, they never skipped a beat. They loved both of their children, and their love for them seemed to make their relationship stronger, bringing them closer together. Skidrow brought them to the club several times a week, sharing his life with his children in every way possible. We all had a special place in our hearts for Dusty. There was something about seeing the world through his eyes that always brought a smile to our faces. He's a great kid, and I knew he was going to be devastated by his father's death. We're all going to have to do our part to make sure he never forgets how much his dad loved him.

"Allie's been with Dallas all afternoon trying to help her out," Guardrail explained. Allie was his Old Lady. They met when Guardrail set out to find her brother, Tony. Guardrail's plan was to use Allie to get to her brother, but he never thought he'd actually fall for her. He did, nonetheless, and Allie is the best thing that ever happened to him.

"Dusty doing ok?" I asked.

"I don't think she's even told him yet. She still needs some time to wrap her head around all of this. Hell, we *all* do," he answered.

"No doubt about that."

"Call me if anything comes up. I'll be back later tonight to check on things."

"No need for that. I've got it. I'll call you if we need you," I told him.

"Thanks," he said as he crossed his arms. "Maverick?"

"Yeah?"

"Henley isn't like the girls around here, and being at the club full time is going to be *different* for her," he said.

"And?"

"Just give her a chance to get accustomed to it. You know, try being... *nice*," he said. He turned and walked away before I had a chance to say anything in response. One of those slow, depressing country songs blared from the jukebox as I grabbed my beer and finished it off. I was sitting the empty bottle down on the counter, when Cassidy walked in with Henley. Cassidy's lips moved a mile a minute as she rambled on and on in Henley's ear, but I could tell from the expression on Henley's face that she wasn't really listening to a word Cass said. I'd seen Henley a couple of times when she came around the club with Cass, but never really made an effort to talk to her. Never really felt the need. She wasn't my type, if I even had a type. But, now I was stuck with her until this mess gets settled. Henley looked over in my direction and seemed to be caught off-guard when she noticed me looking at her. She held my gaze for a moment, captivating me with a soul-searching stare. I was almost disappointed when she turned away.

I watched as she nervously ran her fingers through her long bangs as she unsuccessfully tried to tuck them behind her ear. Cassidy continued to talk as Henley's dark eyes anxiously skirted around the room. Unlike her sister, she wasn't wearing much make-up, but then again, with her olive skin, she really didn't need it. She was a natural beauty. When Cassidy pointed across the room to Boozer, Henley's full lips curved into a smile as she held up her hand and gave him a bashful wave. Her cheeks turned crimson as she quickly dropped her hand to her side and began to fiddle with the hem of her vintage t-shirt. It was obvious that she wasn't exactly comfortable being here, but she would have to realize that we were here to keep her safe. Nothing else really mattered.

My attention was still focused on Henley

when Cooter, one of our prospects, sat down beside me. He let out a deep sigh when his phone chimed with a text message. He grabbed it out of his back pocket and read it, cursing under his breath.

"Damn it. I can't catch a break with her. I mean," he whined. "I love her and all, but fuck."

When I looked over to him, he took it as an invitation to continue with whatever was on his mind.

"I've done everything she's asked me to do, and she's still bitching at me. I've just about decided that you can't make a woman happy," he started as he motioned over to Cassidy for a beer. "She's always on my case about something. It doesn't matter what I do, it's never enough." He stopped long enough to take a drink from his beer before he continued. "I just can't get away from it. You know? Every time I turn around she's calling to ask me… *Are you okay? When are you going to be home?* It never ends. You'd think she'd finally just give it a rest, but *nooo*! She just keeps at it. And it's even worse when I'm home. *When are you going to do this? When are you going to do that?* Man, it just goes on and on."

I looked down at my empty beer and wondered how the hell I got stuck listening to him ramble on like this. I raised my empty beer bottle and waved it in the air letting Cassidy know that I needed another one. When she placed my cold beer on the counter, I noticed Henley walking over to the back of the bar. As I watched her, I realized that she was taller than I'd remembered, and I found myself wondering what she was hiding under that old t-shirt. I imagined her having one of those athletic builds that some girls have without even really trying. She didn't seem like the kind of girl that was into sports as she walked over towards our old Pac Man Arcade game. We'd pulled the damn thing out of some rundown bar downtown, and I hadn't seen anyone even play it since we installed the thing.

"I've done everything she's asked. Hell, I painted her damn bathroom three fucking times before she was happy with it," he carried on, completely oblivious to the fact that I could care less what he was talking about. He took another tug of his beer before he continued, "At least she can cook. Man, she makes the best lasagna you ever put in your mouth. Never found anyone that could make it like hers."

I tried to tune him out as I watched Henley start up the game. When she took the knob in her hand and leaned closer to the screen, her faded blue jean shorts rose slightly, showing off her sexy, long, tan legs. My eyes were zeroed in on her hips swaying from side to side when Cooter's voice pulled me back into his rant.

"You just can't find a good Italian woman

like her anymore. She's one of a kind. I guess that's why I put up with all of her shit. We only get one momma, right? What's a man supposed to do? You know?"

Realizing for the first time that he was actually talking about his mother, pissed me the fuck off. "I wouldn't know. My mother died when I was a kid. I'd say you're lucky to have her," I told him as I turned my head away from him, ignoring whatever he mumbled under his breath. Out of the corner of my eye, I noticed Henley jumping up and down. Her hips jerked from side-to-side as she pumped her fists in the air, obviously celebrating her win over the game. Watching her made me feel lighter somehow, an unlikely diversion from the darkness that usually consumed me. After several seconds of prancing around in the corner, she suddenly stopped and slowly turned her head, peering around the room. Her lips pressed together as she checked to see if anyone had seen her little victory dance. When her eyes locked on mine, she bit her bottom lip. Her mouth slowly curved into a bashful smile as she shrugged her shoulders, acknowledging that she knew I'd seen her. I turned my head and looked away in disbelief.

I sat there for a moment, trying to clear my head, but I couldn't stop myself. I don't know what exactly triggered it... maybe it was that goofy little dance or her adorable smile, but she'd just done something no one has been able to do in months. Henley Gray just made me smile. Fuck.

Chapter 8

HENLEY

WHAT IS IT about those green eyes that captivated me? It just doesn't make any sense. Of course, he's absurdly good looking, with his shaggy brown hair and perfect body, but it's more than that. When I looked at him, I saw something that I just couldn't explain, and it made me want to know more about him. I wanted to know the demons he was fighting… why there was such hurt hidden behind those beautiful emerald eyes.

"Would you like a beer or something?" Boozer asked me, being a gentleman as always.

"No thanks. I'm good."

"How about a game of pool?"

"Trust me… you don't want to play pool with me. I'm beyond *terrible*. It would be like Chinese torture to play against me. Besides, it's been a really long day. I think I'm just going to go crash for the night." I could see the disappointment cross his handsome face when I turned him down. I would've suggested playing a game of darts, but I was exhausted. I just wanted to crawl into bed and forget this day ever happened.

"Maybe some other time, then," he said with a kind smile. "Just let me know if you need anything."

"Thanks Boozer. I really appreciate it." I patted him on the arm and headed over to tell Cassidy that I was going to bed. She was clearing the empty bottles off the counter top as she talked to a couple of the guys sitting at the bar.

"How's it going Lee Bug? Haven't seen much of you tonight. You making it okay?" she asked as she busied herself behind the bar.

"Yep. Hanging in."

"Good. Sorry I haven't been able to spend more time with you. I've been swamped over here. Ellie couldn't make it in tonight, so it's just been me all night."

"Cass, I'm fine. You don't have to worry over me," I assured her.

"Can't help myself. You've been through a lot today," she said with concern. "I still can't get it out of my head. Those guys could have…"

"Don't. Nothing happened. Nothing is going to happen to me. I think it's silly that I am even here. I should be home waiting on my final grades to come in, not hanging out here with the

Hell's Angels."

"Henley, don't say shit like that! You know better than to disrespect these men, especially in their own damn clubhouse. You need them right now. They're the only ones who can keep you safe, and you need to appreciate their…"

I held up my hands in surrender and said, "You're right. You're right. I'm a jerk. I'm sorry. I'm just tired. It's been a hell of a day, and I just need to get some sleep."

"Cotton had a couple of the prospects bring your stuff over from the apartment. I gave them the list of things you wanted, and they set up everything in your room."

"Wow. Well that was nice of them. I'll be sure to thank them tomorrow," I promised.

"And you should know…" she started, but paused to look around the bar before she continued. "I wasn't going to say anything, but someone broke into our apartment. When the guys got there, the entire place had been ransacked."

"What the hell? Who would have done something like that?" I knew the answer before the question ever left my lips.

"They didn't say for sure, but I'm positive it was the guys that tried to break into your car."

"What were they expecting to find in our apartment?" I asked as my heart began to pound nervously against my chest.

"You... or at least something that could lead them to you. Whoever these guys are, they seem pretty intent on finding you, so that's why Cotton put Maverick in charge of watching over you."

It was hard enough being here like this, but I definitely didn't need Mr. Green Eyes watching my every move. He's always so damn serious, with his blank stare and grim expression. It was like someone had just killed his dog or something. I don't think I've ever even seen the man smile, and now he was going to be *watching* over me. *Crap on a cracker.* Just being in the same room with him made me feel all awkward and nervous, and it made my palms sweaty just thinking about it.

"It's his job, Henley. He'll make sure nothing happens to you," she replied.

"I will do what they tell me to do. But I don't need a freaking babysitter, Cassidy. Especially not him."

"Maverick will do whatever it takes to keep you safe. That's all that matters. Even if you don't like it, you're going to have to make this thing work. It's not going to be easy for either of you. You're just going to have to make the best of it," she said, as she started restocking the bar's coolers.

"Damn it all to hell," I told her as I rolled my eyes. "Why did I ever leave the house? I should've just gone to bed and none of this would have ever happened. I wouldn't have to deal with Mr. Grouch."

"Henley, just do what he says. He takes club business very seriously, and it'll only piss him off if you don't do what he tells you," she warned.

"Yeah... well, I'll do what I can to not *piss him off*. Alright?" I asked sarcastically. "I'm going to bed, *mom*. I'll see you in the morning."

As I started to walk out of the bar, I looked over at Maverick. He was sitting alone, drinking another shot of whiskey. His elbows were stretched across the countertop as he stared into the empty shot glass. A part of me wanted to go to him... ask him what was bothering him, but I couldn't get the courage to do it, so I just left.

I still didn't know my way around the entire clubhouse. When Cassidy told me where my room was, I thought I knew exactly where she was talking about. I was wrong. This place was like a maze with all the doors and hallways, but after asking three different guys for help, I finally managed to find my room. When I opened the door, I was pleased to see that Cassidy was right. The guys managed to get everything I asked for and more. One of them even brought my favorite blanket from my bedroom. I took off my clothes and put on my favorite Game of Thrones t-shirt. When I crawled into bed, I was relieved to see that they even remembered to get the pillows off of my bed. I'm a little obsessed with them and knew I wouldn't be able to sleep without them.

"Henley?" a man's voice called with a pounding knock against on my door.

"Hold on," I answered as I got up from the bed and walked towards the door. When I opened it, Maverick was standing there with his overpowering presence and his beautiful green eyes glaring straight at me. He didn't say a word as his eyes dropped down, reading the words on my t-shirt or possibly checking out my boobs. I really couldn't tell.

I cleared my throat, trying to draw his attention back to my face and asked, "Did you need something?"

His eyes slowly meandered down my body, roaming over my bare legs. My feet shifted nervously as he continued to stand there blatantly staring at me. His intense gaze burned against my flesh, making me pull at the hem of my long t-shirt. With a deep sigh, he ran his fingers roughly through his hair, and my eyes instantly zoned in on his waist. His faded blue jeans dropped low around his hips and with his arm lifted, it gave me a peek at his abdomen. My eyes widened when I noticed he had a very pronounced, very sexy V. Damn, I did not need to see that.

His head was still facing down, and I assumed he was checking out my dark purple toenail polish when he asked, "You got every-thing you need?"

"Yep. All good here," I told him as I turned back and looked around the room. My clothes were all hanging in the closet, my make-up was on the small dresser, and my bed was made up with fresh sheets. The guys had done everything they could to make the room as nice as possible. When I turned back to face Maverick, he was still staring at me with a peculiar look on his face. "The guys really did an amazing job here. It was really sweet of them. Did you need something?"

"Good," Maverick said with a nod. "It's late. I just wanted to make sure you were settled, I'll be back in the morning. We have a few things to discuss." Without another word, he turned around and left.

I stood there staring at the empty doorway, wondering what the hell we had to *talk* about. Something told me that he wasn't exactly thrilled about having to keep an eye on me, but the way he just looked at me? Yeah, that was *hot*. This man had me all kinds of confused. I was tempted to just pack up my stuff and get the hell out of here. I told Cotton everything I knew, so there was really no point in me staying.

Chapter 9

MAVERICK

"WHERE THE HELL do you think you're going, Henley?" I growled. I was on my way to the kitchen when I found Henley tiptoeing down the dark hallway, her arms crammed full with all of her shit. An exasperated curse rumbled under her breath as she stopped dead in her tracks. With her hip cocked out to the side, she stared at me with a frustrated pout. Too fucking cute. Her long hair was pulled up high on her head in some kind of bun, with loose strands falling down around her shoulders. Her dark brown eyes looked black as coal as she stood there staring at me, wearing nothing but that damn t-shirt. My eyes trailed down the length of her long, sexy legs, and I instantly imagined them wrapped around me. Damn. This girl was getting under my skin.

"I'm... uhhh... I'm going home?" she sputtered.

"No… you're not. Get your ass back to your room and go to bed," I ordered. There was no way I was letting her leave, at least not yet.

"And why should I do that? I've already told Cotton everything I remembered about the shooting, so there's really no reason for me to stay here," she said, sounding like she actually believed what she was saying.

"What are you going to do when these guys come knocking on your door? Huh? You gonna take care of it on your own? Hit them over the head with one of your fancy fucking pillows? Hear me when I say this, Henley Gray. Once you leave here, there's *no coming back*. No one will be there to help you when they come for that pretty little neck of yours. And let's be clear… *they will* come for you," I warned. A defeated look crossed her face as she stood trying to decide what she was going to do. Then a spark of anger crossed her face when she realized that I was right, making me almost smile with satisfaction.

She glanced up to the ceiling as a frustrated burst of air rushed from her lungs. "Well, thank you for clearing that all up for me, *Maverick*."

"Henley…" I called out to her.

"What?" she snapped.

"You'll be safer here. Club protection is the best thing you've got going right now."

"Whatever you say, **boss**." She rolled her eyes as she turned and walked back into her room, slamming the door behind her. I stood there for a minute listening to her endless stream of profanities as she tossed her things around in her room. A part of me was tempted to go in there and set her straight. Explain what kind of danger she was really in. If she had left here tonight, I have no doubt that they would have found her and killed her. Even though having her here was going to be a pain in my ass, I wouldn't be able to live with myself if something happened to her.

"You lost, Maverick?" Peyton asked playfully. She was one of the club girls. Most of the brothers called them Fury's Felines... pussies that were always eager to please, and Peyton was a club favorite. She had a way with her mouth that could make any man forget the world around him, even if just for a little while.

"Hey, Peyton. You're up late tonight."

"I was just spending a little time with Clutch. He's having a hard time with ... you know... everything. I was trying to cheer him up a bit," she explained. "But he's asleep now, and I was just heading back to my room. Want to join me?"

"Yeah, I'm up for that," I told her as I followed her back to her room. I needed to let off some steam, and Peyton was just the girl to help me out.

"I haven't seen much of you lately," she told me as she hastily began to unbuckle my belt.

Without hesitation, she dropped down to her knees. Her long, black hair fell around her shoulders as her fingers worked to release the zipper of my jeans. "We have some catching up to do, handsome." She smiled up at me, and her brown eyes filled with eagerness, she began lowering my jeans down below my hips. She took me in her hand and brushed her warm wet tongue around the head of my cock. As her hand began to slowly stroke up and down my now hardening shaft, she said "I heard you're going to be around more since you're helping out with Henley and all."

As soon as the sound of Henley's name left her lips, my dick went limp. Fuck. She'd only been here one night, and she was already turning into a cock block. I took a step back and said, "I've got to go."

"What? Baby, we were just getting started. Let me make you feel good…," she whined, her hands dropping down to her side.

"Maybe some other time," I told her as I pulled up my jeans and headed for the door. Still pulling up my zipper, I stepped out into the hall. When I started down the hallway, I found Henley standing in her doorway watching me with a look of disgust on her face that I wasn't expecting. Before I had I chance to say anything to her, she slammed her door and locked it. I almost called out to her, but I stopped myself. I knew there was no reason for me to fucking explain myself to her, but I couldn't shake the feeling of guilt that was scratching at the back of my mind. I decided to ignore it and headed to bed. I was ready for this fucking day to end.

For the next week, Henley did her best to avoid me. Every time we were in the same room, she would make herself busy talking to Cassidy or one of the guys. Even though she wasn't exactly sharing it with me, she always had a beaming smile on her face. It was like she was immune to all the negative shit that was swarming around her. Hell, nothing seemed to get her down. As much as I hated to admit it, I found myself being drawn to her light, and each day I was finding it harder to ignore. From time to time, she would notice me watching her, our eyes locking for just a brief moment before she would smile and turn away. I couldn't help myself, I started to look forward to those smiles.

With everything that was going on at the club, the next few days became a blur. After we buried Skidrow, I spent most of my time working with Big Mike, looking for anything that might help us find the guys that killed Skid. From everything that Henley had told us, we had completely ruled out Tony's old crew. We already knew that they didn't have the manpower to back that kind of threat. It had to be someone else.

Cotton called Henley into his office again. He was getting impatient with the lack of information we'd collected, and he wanted to make sure she'd told us everything she could remember. Unfortunately, she didn't have anything to add to what she'd already told us. We were running out of ideas when Big Mike suggested, "Why don't we use her as bait?"

"Who?"

"Henley. We already know that they want her. They went to all the trouble of putting that tracker on her car. It'd be easy. We could send her back home and wait for them to come after her," he explained. "We could hook her up with a wire and a GPS."

"No."

"Hear me out. We have to do whatever we can to find these guys, and she might be the only option that we have right now. You know we wouldn't let anything happen to her," he promised. "I'd make sure of it."

"Not taking that chance," I growled. I'm sure he wasn't expecting my reaction, but there was no way in hell that I was going to take a chance with Henley's life. It was my job to keep her safe, and I intended to do just that.

"Let's, at least, talk to Cotton about it. See what he thinks," he suggested, not willing to let his idea go.

"Drop it, Mike. It's not going to happen," I told him firmly. "We'll just have to find another way."

Chapter 10

HENLEY

I WAS STARVING. I'd been helping Cassidy with inventory for the past two hours, and I hadn't had a chance to eat. As soon as we finished sorting everything at the bar, I went to the kitchen to see if the guys had anything made up for lunch. When I walked in, the room was empty except for Maverick. He was sitting all alone at the long, kitchen table with a not-so-subtle scowl on his face. I wondered what he was thinking about, sitting there alone in the quiet. He was in a daze, totally unaware that I had even walked into the room. When I looked at him, I could see a world of hurt hidden behind those beautiful green eyes. He sat there slumped down in his chair, and I could almost see the weight of the world sitting on his broad shoulders. He was completely lost in his own thoughts, and it didn't look like a place anyone needed to be.

Trying to knock him out of his stupor, I sat

down beside him and asked, "Do you ever smile?" He let out a deep sigh of frustration, making sure I knew he wasn't exactly thrilled that I was interrupting his lunch. He didn't even acknowledge my question as he took a big bite of his ham sandwich.

"Seriously, does anything make you happy, or are you always such a grouch?" I pushed, trying to get some kind of reaction out of him.

"Are you bored, Henley? Trying to pick a fight with me so you'll have something to occupy your time?" he asked with his mouth full.

"I just don't get it. You're a good-looking guy, the new Sergeant of Arms of the club, and the guys seem to really respect you."

"So, you're *flirting* with me now?" he asked, looking over to me with a sexy smirk. Damn. That smile could melt hearts from a mile away.

"Oh please, don't flatter yourself. I'm just trying to get inside that head of yours."

"Don't," he barked. "You don't know shit about me, and…"

"That's not exactly true. I know you have a son. A son you loved enough to give him up, so he could have a life you didn't think you could give him on your own." His eyebrows furrowed as he glared at me, but he didn't try to stop me from continuing. "And I know that had to be hard – really hard, but you didn't let it stop you. You kept living, working to make your club better… safer. I also know that you helped your brother get in that other club in Tennessee, even though you probably wanted him to be here with you. You did it, because it was the best thing for *him*."

"Cassidy talks too damn much," he grumbled.

"You're missing the point," I snapped.

"What's the point then, Henley? Tell me. What exactly do you think I should be smiling about?" he said as he glared at me angrily, warning me to shut the hell up, but I was determined to make my point.

"As far as I can tell you have plenty to smile about, but you're focusing on the wrong things. You have to learn from your mistakes and let the past go. Just live your life the best way that you can and forget about the things that you can't change. Don't be so hard on yourself about everything. Lighten up," I explained, wishing that he would actually listen to what I was saying.

"The past makes us who we are. I live it and breathe it. It's not something I can just let go of," he said as he turned his attention back to his sandwich.

"That may be true, Maverick, but you can either dwell on your own misery or try to find your way back to some kind of happiness. You just have to take that first step."

"Maybe, just maybe, I don't want to take that

step. Maybe I like things just the way they are." His green eyes darkened with the anguish that churned inside of him. I wanted to reach out and hold him in my arms. Take all his pain away. I had to find a way to make him see things differently, to distract him from his despair, even if it's just for a little while. I have to try to get him to take that first step.

"We'll just have to see about that," I told him smiling.

"Just leave it alone, Henley," he said, his voice full of irritation, all of which was directed at me.

"Don't be such a grump. I might just end up surprising you," I told him as I stood up. "I'm going with Cassidy to see Dallas."

"You're not going alone," he snapped, dropping his sandwich down on his plate.

"I won't be alone. I'm going with Cassidy."

"You don't go anywhere without a member of this club. Period. I've got to meet with Cotton, so I'll get Clutch to go with you. Go straight there and back. No stops," he said firmly.

"Whatever you say, boss." I gave a quick salute as I turned to leave.

When I finally made it outside, Cassidy was already waiting for me in her car. The engine was running while she sat there talking on her phone. When I got in the car, she brought her finger up to her lips, letting me know not to say anything.

"Yes, sir. I'll tell her," she said with her voice oozing with sweetness. I knew right away that she was talking with Dad. "Yeah, she got her scores last night. I think she aced them all," she said as she rolled her eyes at me. She wanted to act like she didn't care about my grades, but I knew she was proud of me. "I love you too, Daddy. I'll have her call you as soon as she gets home. Talk to you later," she said as she hung up the phone.

"Did you tell him about what happened?" I asked, praying that she had enough sense not to worry him.

"Of course not. You know how he overreacts about stuff."

"Good. You ready to go?" I asked, trying to change the subject.

"Yeah, we better get going. I don't want to be late," she said as she slipped the car into reverse.

I'd made plans with her to go over and help babysit Dallas' kids, so she could take care of some things with her lawyer. Apparently, her insurance company was giving her a hard time about her husband's life insurance policy, and they didn't want to give her the full pay out. Her family really needed that money, and she had to do whatever she could to make sure they got it.

When we got to her house, Clutch parked his bike in the street out front. I thought he would follow us inside, but he stayed put. He was just sitting there, watching us. I gave him a quick wave as we got out of the car, but I got nothing in return. When I noticed the serious look on his face, I wondered if he was pissed that he had to come. I wondered if he thought it was as ridiculous as I did that he even had to be here.

"Don't worry about it, Henley. He's just doing his job," Cassidy assured me as she shut her car door.

"I feel bad. He doesn't look like he wants to be here and," I started.

"*Henley*, stop fretting over Clutch, and let's get inside. Dallas is waiting for us," she urged.

I looked back towards the house and saw that Dallas was already waiting for us at the front door. It was a great little ranch style house with white rockers on the front porch and a big shop in the back. Cassidy told me that Guardrail's construction company helped her husband build the house several years ago, just before Dusty was born. In the front yard, there was an amazing treehouse with swings and a slide and several bicycles were scattered on the grass.

"Thank you both for coming. I appreciate it more than you could ever know," Dallas said as she picked up her purse and keys from the side table. "I shouldn't be long. I think I just have to sign some papers or something, and then, I'll be back."

"There's no rush. Take your time," Cassidy told her. "We've been looking forward to babysitting."

"They're hanging out in Dusty's room playing video games. That should keep them entertained for a little while, and there's sandwich stuff in the kitchen if they get hungry," Dallas explained. "Call me if anything comes up."

"We'll be fine," I assured her.

As soon as Dallas pulled out of the driveway, Cassidy said, "I'll go make up some lunch for them. You go make sure they aren't up to anything."

"Gotcha," I said as I went in search of Dusty's room. Considering everything that had happened, the house was extremely neat and organized. Everything seemed to have its place. As I walked through the house, the walls were filled with pictures of their family, and each photo told its own story. They were happy, and it broke my heart to see such a precious family destroyed by such a malicious act. Those men really had no idea what that one night, that one act of violence took away from this family. I was looking at one of the most recent pictures of the kids sitting on Skidrow's motorcycle when the sounds of the children's voices rumbled down the hallway. When I peeked my head through the doorway, both of them stopped what they were doing and looked at me with mischief in their eyes. I wasn't sure what was going on, but I'd been around enough kids to know something was going on.

"So, what are you guys up to?" I asked smiling. They looked so adorable sitting there together side by side with their video game controllers in their hands. Looking at them made it hard for me to believe that they would ever misbehave.

"Playing Batman. We're trying to get the bad guys, but Katie won't do it right," Dusty complained. His nose crinkled with frustration as he looked over at his sister.

"I *am* doing it right, Dusty. Stop being such a twerp," Katie protested. Her face flashed red with anger as she tossed the controller towards Dusty. "You do it. This game is stupid anyway." She stood up and started for the door. Dusty watched her walk out of the room, his long blonde hair falling into his eyes, almost covering the tiny freckles that dappled the bridge of his nose. I had always heard that Down's children were extremely lovable and happy, and Dusty certainly fit that description.

"Don't go, Katie. I wanna play wif' you," he pleaded. The sound of his little voice tugged at my heart, and I wished Katie would come back to finish the game. I remember what it was like when Cassidy and I would argue over little things like our Barbie dolls and tea sets. It always killed me when she would storm out of the room, leaving me to play all alone. Dusty was ten years old, and he clearly enjoyed playing with his older sister.

Regrettably, she was officially a teenager with a short fuse and wasn't willing to listen to him. "We've been playing that stupid game for over an hour, Dusty. I need a *break*," she huffed just before slamming her bedroom door. I felt certain that it wasn't just the video game that was getting to Katie, so I decided to distract Dusty in hopes of giving her some time to cool off. I walked over to him and placed my hand on top of his head, drawing his attention away from Katie.

"Cassidy is making up some sandwiches for lunch. Are you hungry?"

"Is it Peanut butter and jelly?" Dusty asked.

"If that's what you want, I'm sure Cassidy will make you one."

"Yay! That's what I want and wif' lots of chips… and one of those cherry popsicles, if I clean my plate," he declared, his eyes bright with excitement.

"You got it," I answered. His face lit up, and his argument with Katie was totally forgotten. He raced for the kitchen, his little feet clomping on the floor, and sat at the table. A wide smile spread across his face as he watched Cassidy fix his plate. So freaking cute. Happiness radiated off of him, making it impossible not to smile right along with him.

"Yum," he hummed as soon as Cassidy sat his sandwich and chips down in front of him. He grabbed a few chips and shoved them in his mouth. Knowing that he was distracted, I went to go check on Katie.

When I tapped on her door, she mumbled, "Come in."

"You ok?" I asked. I should've left her alone, especially since I didn't know her very well, but I've never been the type to just leave things alone. She was laying on her bed listening to her iPod.

"I'm fine…. I'm sorry about earlier," Katie whispered, pulling the headphones from her ears. "I've just got a lot on my mind, and there's only so much Batman I can take."

"Totally understandable. You've had a lot to deal with over the last couple of weeks. I know it's been hard," I told her as I sat on the corner of the bed. "Hopefully things will get better soon."

"I shouldn't have been mean to Dusty. He's having a hard time, too. I just get frustrated with those stupid games. He wants me to win all the time, and I just can't."

"Did you know that Batman has some pretty cool cheats? It would make it a lot easier to play it, if you used them."

"I've heard about them, but I've never really

known how to do it."

"It isn't hard, and you can find most of them online. It will let you change Batman's outfits and skins. You can even choose alternate endings. They aren't hard to do, and if you want me to, I could show you how to do it," I offered.

"That'd be so cool. I'm sure Dusty would love it, and I know he could use the distraction. Daddy's death has really been hard on him. He just doesn't understand why he isn't coming home. I've tried to explain it to him, but he just keeps expecting him to come walking through the front door," she said, her voice cracked as tears began to pool in her eyes.

"I'm sure it's hard on all of you, but in time, it'll get better. You'll always miss him. But eventually you'll be able to find comfort in knowing that your dad loved you both very much, and he'd be here with you if he could."

"It's just hard, you know? I'm used to seeing him every single day, and now… he's just gone. I didn't even get to tell him goodbye. I know people say that stuff all the time, but I just wish I had five more minutes with him. I don't know what to do anymore," she cried with tears shimmering in her eyes.

Seeing her in pain, the tears now streaming down her precious face, made my heart hurt for her. Her tear soaked eyes looked up at me when I put my hand on her shoulder and said, "You move *forward*. It's the only direction God really gives us."

She nodded with understanding and wiped the tears from her cheeks. I leaned over and gave her a quick hug, before I stood up and said, "Let's grab something to eat, and then I'll show you some cool tricks to use the next time you play Batman with Dusty."

"Thanks, Henley. That'd be awesome," she said as she followed me to the kitchen. After we ate, we spent the next hour going over the cheats I knew for the games they had. We were all sitting around the TV cheering Katie on when Dallas came home. She stopped in his doorway and smiled when she found us huddled on the floor together.

"Did you get it worked out?" Cassidy asked as she pulled herself up off the floor.

"I think so. The lawyer said if nothing else comes up I should have my check by the end of the week."

"That's great, Dallas. I'm sure you're re- lieved," I told her as Cassidy reached out her hand and helped me up.

"You have no idea. Daniel always paid all the bills, so I'm a little overwhelmed," her eyes dropped to the ground as she got lost in the memory of her husband.

"I could help you if you need it," I offered. "I'm pretty good with numbers."

"Really? That would be great. I need all the help I can get right now, and thanks again for coming today. It really helped me out."

"Can they come back and play wif' me?" Dusty interrupted, jumping up and down with excitement.

"Of course they can, buddy. Someday real soon, but right now, I need to head over to the clubhouse for a bit. I just talked to Clutch, and he said they could fix the car if I brought it over to the garage. It's been making that funny noise again," she explained. I'd forgotten that he was even here until she said his name. I looked out the window towards the front yard, and he was still sitting there on his bike, doing his thing, and he still didn't look happy about being there.

"Awesome. Can I go wif' you?" Dusty begged.

"You have to be a good boy… no touching anything," she warned.

"I pomis'." His face lit up when he realized that she was going to let him go. I was glad that he still had that part of his dad. The club would always be there for him.

"Can I stay here?" Katie asked. "I want to try the rest of these tricks that Henley gave me."

"No, Katie. I'm not leaving you alone, at least, not yet," her mother said as she placed her arm around Katie's shoulder, pulling her close to her chest.

"We better get going," I told them, heading towards the door.

Cassidy and I gave them each a hug before we left. As we were pulling out of their driveway, I thought about how ironic today had actually been. We were there to help them out and to raise their spirits, but I left there feeling better than I had in weeks.

Chapter 11

MAVERICK

"DUSTY! PUT THAT down," Dallas scolded. "You know you aren't supposed to touch anything in here." She took the wrench from his hand and wiped the grease off of his little fingers. I'd gone out back to the garage to see Clutch. I went to ask how things went with Henley, and found him with his head under the hood of Dallas's car. He was always working on someone's engine, and I wondered why he didn't have a garage of his own.

My phone chimed with a text message, but I ignored it, leaving it in my pocket. Dallas had already noticed me walking up, and she looked relieved to see me. She smiled and said, "Look, Dusty! Maverick's here."

"Mav-wrick!" he shouted as he raced over in my direction with his arms spread wide. I bent down and tried to brace myself for his impact, but still almost fell backwards when he jumped into my arms.

I lifted him up and said, "Hey there, little brother. Are you giving your mom a hard time?" I noticed Katie sitting in the corner with her face glued to her phone, and I wondered if she even knew I was there.

"No sir," he said shaking his head. "I'm being good." I looked over to Dallas, and she shrugged her shoulders and smiled as she turned back to Clutch to see what he was doing with the car.

"You want to go to the kitchen and see if there's any ice cream?"

"Yes! I want cookie dough ice cream. It's my fav-rit'," he explained. His little body began to wiggle with excitement. I lowered him to the ground and started walking towards the back door. "We'll be right back," I called out to Dallas.

"Just a little, Dusty. We haven't had dinner yet," she ordered.

"Okay," he said as he reached up and took a hold of my hand.

Just as we were leaving the garage, Dusty shouted, "Hey Henwey!" Lifting his free hand up high, he began waving frantically in her direction. She was helping Cassidy carry some empty boxes to the dumpster.

She stopped with her arms loaded with cardboard boxes and shouted, "Hey Dusty!" Her face beamed with a wide smile, and I knew right then that they'd had a good day together.

"I'm gonna go get some ice kem' with Mav-wrick," he told her with the biggest grin I'd ever seen.

Still smiling, she said, "Save some for me!"

"I will. Momma said I can only have a little since I haven't ate dinner yet." His little finger clutched tightly around my fingers as I led him into the kitchen. I reached under his arms and lifted him up on to the counter by the refrigerator. He sat there, swinging his feet out and kicking the cabinet with the back of his heels, as I dug in the freezer looking for his cookie dough ice cream. He eagerly watched as I placed several spoonfuls into the bowl.

"Thanks, Mav-wrick'," Dusty said with his eyes trained on his bowl of ice cream. "Ummm, you have sprinkles?"

"Sorry, buddy. I don't, but I'll make sure to get some for next time."

After handing him the bowl, I lifted him up and carried him over to the table. "Did you have fun today with Henley and Cassidy?"

"Hen-wey is cool. She saved Gotham City for me," he said eyeing his bowl of ice cream. He grabbed his spoon, and brought a big bite up to his mouth. "Yum! It's good."

My phone chimed with another text message, but I continued to ignore it. When it beeped two more times, Dusty said, "Your phone beeps a lot. I think someone wants you."

"I'll check it later. Eat up, mister. Your mom is waiting for us." I already knew that the messages weren't important. I'd been getting the same ones over and over, and I was about to lose my patience.

I watched as Dusty shoveled bite after bite into his mouth. He made all these funny little humming and grunting noises as he ate. He was obviously enjoying every damn spoonful. As soon as he finished his ice cream, I took him back to Dallas. Clutch was just about done with the car, and they were getting ready to leave.

On my way back inside, my phone beeped again, and I went straight to Big Mike's room. I was ready to throw the damn thing out the fucking window, and he was the only one I knew who could fix it.

"Something is wrong with this piece of shit phone," I told him. "I need you to look at it to see if you can fix it."

"What's it doing?" Big Mike asked as he took the phone from my hand.

"I keep getting these stupid text messages, and I can't get them to stop," I explained. "It must be a virus or something."

"These phones don't get viruses, Mav. Let me see what you're talking about." I pointed to one of the messages that had been bombarding my phone over the past twenty-four hours.

Unknown caller: Dogs are capable of understanding up to 250 words and gestures, can count up to five, and can perform simple mathematical calculations. The average dog is as intelligent as a two-year-old child.

Thank you for signing up for *All About Canines*. To Unsubscribe reply "Unsubscribe"

Me: Unsubscribe

Unknown caller: Message unrecognized

Unknown caller: It is a myth that dogs are color blind. They can actually see in color, just not as vividly as humans. It is similar to our vision at dusk.

Thank you for signing up for *All About Canines*. To Unsubscribe reply "Unsubscribe"

Me: Unsubscribe now!

Unknown caller: Unable to retrieve messages at this time

Unknown caller: A dog's mouth exerts 150-200 pounds of pressure per square inch.

Thank you for signing up for *All About Canines*. To Unsubscribe reply "Unsubscribe"

Me: Stop fucking texting me!

Unknown caller: Are you sure you want to stop your subscription of *All About Canines*. You know they are Man's best friend.

Me: Yes

Unknown caller: Command not recognized.

"See what I mean? I can't get this shit to stop, and there are at least six different sites sending me these fucking messages," I shouted with frustration.

"Are you sure you didn't sign up for something?" he asked laughing. "There must be some reason they are sending them to you."

"No, I didn't sign up for shit! Just fix it or get me a new damn phone!"

"Give me a few minutes, and I'll see what I can figure out," he told me as he plugged my phone up to his computer. After a few clicks, he turned to me with a knowing smile on his face.

"Looks like someone was messing with you, man," he chuckled as he handed me back my phone.

"Who the fuck was it?" I demanded to know. "I'll wring his fucking neck!" I looked down at my phone and was tempted to throw it against the damn wall.

"Maverick, I'm sure she didn't mean anything by it. It was just…" he started.

"She? Ahh… fucking hell. *Henley*! It was Henley, wasn't it?" I growled, turning to leave before he responded. He didn't have to answer. I knew it was her. Just thinking about all those damn messages about dogs and cats made my teeth hurt.

"Henley!" I shouted as I headed down the main hall towards her room. "*Hen... ley*!"

I banged on her door and continued to shout until Guardrail came up to me and said, "Hey man, she's out back with Cassidy. What's going on?"

"Nothing I can't handle," I snapped.

"You got a minute? Cotton wants to see us in his office."

"Yeah," I answered, just as my phone chimed with another fucking text message.

Unknown Caller: A group of cats is called a clowder, a male cat is called a tom, a female cat is called a molly or queen while young cats are called kittens.

Thank you for subscribing to Funny Facts about Cats. To unsubscribe reply 'Unsubscribe.'

Me: Henley... knock it off!

Unknown Caller: Response Not Recognized

Me: You are going to pay for this shit

"What's that all about?" Guardrail asked as he looked down at my phone.

"Don't ask," I groaned as I shoved it into my back pocket and followed him into Cotton's office. Cotton was sitting at his desk, sorting through all the papers that were scattered around him.

"What's going on?" I asked.

"We had some trouble on today's run," he grumbled as he dropped the papers on his desk. "The guys were ambushed. Even with the extra manpower, we almost lost the shipment."

"What the fuck?" I asked. "What happened?"

"Boozer said they were loading the crates into the SUV when one of the prospects saw several men watching from one of the empty warehouses. At first it seemed like they were just watching, taking pictures or some shit like that. But then shots were fired, and everyone scattered. Thankfully, no one was hurt," Cotton explained.

"Was it the same guys?" I asked.

"Possibly. Boozer said he'd never seen them before. They were wearing all black, no patches or cuts, but several had the same snake tattoo Henley mentioned." Cotton rubbed the back of his neck, trying to ease the tension growing in his shoulders as he continued.

"What's with the pictures?" I asked.

"I'd say, for whatever reason, they're gathering intel on us. I'm calling church tonight. We're going to buckle down and find out who these fuckers are once and for all."

"I'll let the guys know," Guardrail told him. "Are you calling for a lock down?"

"Not yet, but I don't want anyone taking any unnecessary chances. Until we get a better idea of who is coming at us, we need to be prepared for anything. I have a feeling that these guys are just getting started," he continued.

After leaving Cotton's office, I followed Guardrail out to the parking lot. He hadn't been around much, and I wanted to see what was going on with him.

"How are you making out with Henley?" he asked as he got on his bike.

"She's a pain in the ass. Nothing like I thought she'd be, but I'm getting a handle on her. What about you? How's the new addition on the house?" He'd been remodeling one of those historical houses for over a year, and now that he and Allie were getting married, he was even more determined to finish it. He wanted it done before their wedding this fall.

"*Slow*," he grumbled. "Just haven't had the time to work on it like I've wanted to. Between this mess with the club and finishing up the youth center project – hell, there's just not enough time in the day."

"You'll get it done. You always do, besides the wedding is still a few months away."

"You know I want it perfect for her. She's been through so much, and I want her to be happy."

"She's been living with you for months, and

she's crazy about the place. You don't have to do much to make it a home, and then, she'll wanna fill it up with a bunch of rug-rats," I laughed. A year ago, I wouldn't have imagined Kane having kids of his own, but since he met Allie, he's changed. Now, he wants nothing more than to fill that house with their children.

"We will. I'll make sure of it. Things are heating up around here. Make sure Henley understands that," he warned. Just as the words came out of his mouth, my phone chimed with another text message. I pulled it out of my pocket and read the message.

> **Unknown caller:** Did you know that for its weight, spider web silk is actually stronger and tougher than steel.
>
> Thank you for subscribing to Crazy Facts about Spiders. To unsubscribe, reply 'unsubscribe.'
>
> **Me:** Henley – you've been warned
>
> **Unknown caller:** Message failed to be recognized

"For fucks sake," I groaned as I returned my phone to my back pocket.

"Henley?"

"None other."

"She giving you a hard time? Can't handle sweet, little Henley?" he laughed out loud.

"Oh…I'll handle her. You can count on that," I huffed as I went in search of my little trouble maker.

Chapter 12

HENLEY

"**D**USTY LOOKED SO happy with Maverick," I told Cassidy as she tossed another bag into the large garbage bin.

"Yeah, all the guys seem to have a soft spot for him. I can't really blame them. He's an awesome kid."

"It makes me feel a little bad for messing with Maverick so much over the last couple of days," I confessed. A part of me wondered if I was going too far, but I couldn't seem to stop myself.

"You need to lay off before you really piss him off," Cassidy warned as I closed the lid on the dumpster.

"You're no fun, sis. It's just a few text messages," I smirked, following her back into the bar. It was pretty quiet except for a few of the guys sitting at the back table drinking a beer. They were having an intense conversation and didn't even look up when we walked in.

"Henley, I think something bad happened with the club today. Everyone is on edge. You better lay off for a little while."

"Maybe, but," I told her smiling as I sat down at the bar, watching her start to take inventory.

"*Henley*... what did you do?" she probed.

"Well... let's just say that the little stop we made on the way home from Dallas's house wasn't for me."

"You mean the drugstore? You said you needed tampons," she said, placing her hands on her hips.

"I did, but I may have bought a few other things while I was in there," I told her shrugging my shoulders.

She let out a deep disapproving sigh and said, "Oh god, Henley. He's going to blow a gasket."

"Probably. I'd love to be a fly on the wall when he goes into that bathroom. It's going to be *savage*," I told her as I laughed so loud several of the guys turned to look at me.

"Well, don't come crying to me when he ..."

"*Henley*," Maverick roared behind my back.

My heart started to race at the sound of my name rolling off of his tongue. I didn't have to turn around to know that he was furious with me. I could hear it in his voice.

The subtle hint of cologne and leather

whirled around me, as I turned to face him. Smiling at him with my most innocent smile, I said, "Hey there, Maverick. How's it going?" The closeness of his body next to mine made my knees begin to tremble, but I did my best to ignore my traitorous body.

He stepped closer, his face inches from mine and said, "No more of your bullshit, Henley. No more fucking text messages and no more of that shit you put in my bathroom." I was right. He was pissed.

"I have no idea what you're talking about," I said, trying to hold back my laughter.

"You know *exactly* what I'm talking about. There's going to be hell to pay if you don't stop this shit right now!" he growled, glaring at me with rage in his eyes. Even though his reaction wasn't exactly what I was going for, at least I'd distracted him from his world of gloom and doom for a little while.

"*Well…* just so you know, Preparation H isn't just for hemorrhoids anymore. Lots of people use it for wrinkle cream. You might try it on those little crow's feet you're getting in the corner of your eyes from all that scowling you've been doing," I told him as I grazed my teeth over my bottom lip, still trying my best not to laugh in his face. He slowly drug both his hands down his face, trying to contain his frustration, which made it even more challenging for me not to continue. I just couldn't help myself.

"And you know fiber is really good for your digestive system. It might help regulate your…"

"You think your pretty slick, don't you?" he said. The expression on his face was slowly beginning to change, softening just a bit. A wave of satisfaction washed over me when I realized I was getting to him. As he stepped closer to me, he lifted his hand up to my face and tucked a loose strand of my hair behind my ear. "You should know something, Henley."

"What's that?" I whispered, feeling my knees weaken by the slight touch of his hand.

"Pay back's a *bitch*," he told me with a panty-melting wink. A little shiver of anticipation crept down my spine while I stood there looking at him with that sexy smirk on his face. That smile could bring a girl to her knees, and I would do just about anything to keep it right there on his handsome face.

"Bring it on," I told him as I put on my brave front and walked out of the room. I couldn't help but wonder if he really had it in him to get me back and just how far he'd be willing to go, but I looked forward to finding out.

I managed to talk Cassidy into letting me use her laptop. Over the past few days, I'd been obsessed with searching for practical jokes. I tried a few on Maverick. Vaseline on his door knob, a sexy male model poster hanging over his bed, and changing all his radio stations to Rap. I kept waiting for him to call me out or get me back, and I was a little disappointed when he had no reaction whatsoever to any of it. I was busy searching for my next big stunt when there was a knock on my door. When I opened it, I was surprised to see Guardrail standing there.

"Hey, Kane. How's it going?" I asked, wondering what I'd done to have the VP come knocking at my door.

"Allie's going to babysit Dusty tonight, and she wanted to know if you'd like to go with her."

"Sure! I'd love to," I told him as I quickly closed the laptop.

"She's waiting for you out front. I'll let Maverick know where you are, and I'll send one of the brothers along with you to keep an eye on things."

"Great. Thanks for asking me. I'll be right out." I pulled my hair up into a ponytail and grabbed my purse before heading out front to meet Allie. When I got there, Maverick was busy talking to several of the prospects. They were all intently listening to whatever he was saying; however, his mouth stopped moving the moment he saw me heading in their direction. There was a mischievous twinkle in his eye as he watched me walk over to Allie, and it made me wonder what they were talking about. I was still staring at him when Allie called out to me.

"Hey, Henley. You ready to roll?" Allie asked while she pulled her long hair up into a messy bun. She was wearing a short pencil skirt and high heels, and her smile was bright and welcoming. I could see why Guardrail was so smitten with her.

"You bet. Thanks for asking me to tag along. I needed to get out of that place for a little while," I told her as I got in the passenger seat of her car.

"Girl, I know. There's only so much testosterone a girl can take!" she said laughing.

"Testosterone and sweat!" I snorted.

We were both still laughing when we pulled out of the driveway, but my smile faded when I spotted Maverick. His green eyes were focused completely on me as he continued to talk to the prospects. The minute he was out of my line of sight, I found myself longing to be back there, looking at him and watching his every move. Damn. What was wrong with me? Was I really turning into one of those crazy stalker ladies that drool over some guy who wasn't even interested in them? Yep. I had a thing for the Grinch.

I was relieved to have a distraction from Maverick, even if it was for only a few hours. We spent the night playing Candy Land and Hungry Hippo with Dusty. Allie and I were completely out of practice, and Dusty won every single game. Seeing the smile on his face made me want to keep playing, even after Dallas came home.

I really enjoyed having the time to get to know Allie better. She was so easy to talk to, and her eyes sparkled when she told me about the youth center that Guardrail was building for her company. Now that it was almost complete, she was planning a huge grand opening celebration. Between that and her upcoming wedding, I couldn't imagine her being any happier.

"I have my final fitting for my dress next week. Would you mind going with me? Tell me what you think? I really need an honest opinion," Allie asked.

"I'm sure it will be perfect, but I would love to go with you."

"Great. I'll let Kane know so he can get it worked out with Maverick."

"He'll want to send the cavalry along with us. Hope you're okay with that," I warned her.

"Girl, I'm used to it. I'm lucky if I can go to the grocery store without someone tagging along. But after everything that happened with Tony, I like knowing that he's looking out for me," she explained.

"Actually sounds kind of nice when you put it like that," I confessed.

"When you find someone who loves you enough to put your life before their own, there's nothing like it in the world. I never thought I would find it, but now that I have, I'm going to hold on to it." I could see the love in her eyes as she spoke of their relationship. I found myself wanting that kind of love.

When we pulled through the gates of the clubhouse, things were oddly quiet. After making plans to meet Allie after lunch tomorrow, I headed inside. I couldn't figure out where everyone had gone. Usually the place was humming with the guys moving about and music blaring from the bar. I considered myself lucky to have a quiet night and headed to my room for a hot shower.

When I turned the doorknob, I heard a strange rustle behind my door. Thinking maybe someone was in there, I quickly swung my door open. Before I could move out of the way, a gazillion packing peanuts came barreling into the hall, covering my feet and ankles in white. I stood there frozen, stunned by the mountain of styrofoam pieces that filled my room. There wasn't a place where I could look that wasn't covered.

"What the hell?" I screeched as they continued to cascade down through the doorway.

My attention was instantly drawn over to a dark corner at my left when Maverick purposefully cleared his throat. Gloating, he stood with his arms crossed, wearing the sexiest smile I have ever seen in my life. Just looking at him, with his childlike expression of pure satisfaction, made me want to wrap my arms around him. I should've been pissed. I should've wanted to scream and yell at him, but seeing that look on his face was worth every single little piece of styrofoam in that room.

"*You* did this?" I asked laughing as I pointed towards the huge mess in my room.

He nodded, still smiling with pride.

I looked back at my room for just a brief moment, making sure that I wasn't dreaming. Styrofoam crunched beneath my feet as I walked over to him and said, "You're pretty proud of yourself, aren't you?"

"Yep," he snickered.

"I have to admit," I said, motioning towards my room, "*that* is pretty impressive." He remained silent as I continued, "I mean that took some *time*. I bet you enjoyed planning this all out. Thinking of the perfect way to get me back and waiting for just the right time." I stopped talking when he took a step closer to me.

"I did." His voice was raspy and deep as he inched closer to me. My knees trembled ever so slightly as the warmth of his breath caressed my neck. "All the time it took to get those damn things shoved into your room. It was worth every second to see the look on your face when you opened that door," he whispered.

My eyes drifted down to his perfect round lips. Unable to stop myself, I leaned into him and pressed my mouth against his. His arms immediately wrapped around my waist, pulling me closer to him. A light moan vibrated through my chest as his tongue gently ran across my bottom lip. I couldn't hide my attraction to him any longer, not from him, not from myself. His hands slowly reached up to the sides of my face as I opened my mouth to him. The kiss became demanding, sending an involuntary shudder down my spine. This man had consumed my thoughts, my dreams, my very existence for weeks, and now, in this moment, he was consuming my heart. His scent, his touch, the heat of his body next to mine. I wanted all of him. My hands roamed across his broad chest, feeling his muscles tighten as he continued to claim me with his mouth. I wanted to remember everything about this moment. The feel of his hands against my body. The taste of him against my tongue. Every miniscule detail about this moment would be locked away forever in my memory. Without me even realizing it, Maverick had claimed my heart, and I couldn't help but wonder what he would do with it.

With my back pressed against the wall, he pulled back, releasing me from our embrace and repeated, "Worth every damn second."

Chapter 13

MAVERICK

I'D BEEN SITTING at the bar for over an hour watching Henley and Cassidy carry out an endless line of garbage bags from her room. She'd slowly lost that adorable smile that she was wearing last night, and now she was pouting. Each time she walked past me, her look of irritation grew. I wanted to stop her and pull her close to me so I could feel her lips against mine. I wanted to feel her go limp in my arms, and make her smile like she did last night. Before I could call out to her, Guardrail came and sat down beside me.

"Are you enjoying yourself?" Guardrail asked as he watched them walk out the back door.

"Not as much as I thought I would," I confessed.

"You could've had the prospects help her," he suggested.

"Yeah, but where is the fun in that?" I asked

as my eyes involuntarily wandered to the back door, waiting for her to come back in.

"Ahhh, brother... she's getting to you," he told me with a knowing smile.

"She's a pain in the ass." Even as I said the words, I knew I didn't mean it. I couldn't even look at her without thinking of her lips on mine. That one moment of being with her made the hell I had been going through just seem to fade into a distant memory.

"Been awhile since I've seen you like this, brother. Pain in the ass or not... she's been good for you," he stated. He stood, resting his hand on my shoulder, and said, "Get the prospects to finish cleaning up that mess you made."

Knowing that I had put it off long enough, I picked up my phone and ordered Cooter to get it done. "Cooter's on it."

"Big Mike has been in contact with other clubs in the area. So far, we're the only target, but that isn't really a surprise. We all know that we are the only ones capable of trafficking on a large scale. There has to be a connection we're missing," he explained.

"I think we've been looking at this all wrong. I don't think this is about some pissed off club trying to get back at us," I told him. "These motherfuckers don't give a damn about us or our club. These guys are after our territory."

"And?" Guardrail questioned.

"It's time for us to figure out who is looking to take over our claim on Clallam County. It's a prime location for illegal distribution with all the different ports along the coast. Any idiot could look at a map and see that. We just need to find out who is looking for a new place to move their product."

"I'll talk to Cotton. We'll get Big Mike to do some digging and see what he can come up with," he said as he stood to leave.

After talking with Guardrail, Cotton called us all into church. It didn't take long for him to explain everything to the guys. They all agreed that the chances of someone trying to take over our territory was a real possibility, but finding out who wasn't going to be easy. Cotton planned to get Nitro to look into things on his end, see if he could find any leads.

I was on my way to find Henley when my phone vibrated in my pocket. I was surprised to see that it was Lily calling. I hadn't heard from her in a few weeks, making me worried that something might be wrong.

"Lily?" I asked.

"Hey, Maverick. How are you?"

"I'm fine. Is everything okay with John Warren?" I asked, unable to hide the panic in my voice.

"Yes, he's fine. He's doing great… growing like a weed. He's practically taken over the place—walking, climbing, running. He never stays put," she said laughing. I could hear the love in her voice when she spoke of him, reassuring me once again that he was exactly where he needed to be.

"Good." My chest tightened at the thought of seeing him again. There was so much that I'd missed, and I hated myself for not checking on him more. I should've wanted to know everything about him. I should have, but I couldn't. Instead, I pushed it in the back of my mind, trying to forget, trying to pretend that none of it ever happened. It was just easier that way, easier not to think about what an asshole I really was. "Is there a reason you called, Lily?"

"You know how I told you a few weeks ago that we're trying to get everything finalized with the adoption? Well, now they're really pushing for a DNA test. I thought the birth certificate would be enough, but they want to be sure. Would you mind…" she started.

"When?"

"If it's okay with you, I was thinking you could come here to do it. Then you could spend some time with John Warren. They said we could get the results within twenty-four hours, so you could sign the papers while you were here," she explained. "I know that's asking a lot, but…"

"I'll come as soon as I can. If I can work it out, I'll leave tonight," I told her.

"That would be great. I know John Warren would love to see you, and maybe you could spend some time with Gavin while you were here."

I hadn't seen Gavin since the day he left for Tennessee. We'd spoken on the phone a few times, and the way he talked about working in the garage and prospecting for their club, let me know that he'd made the right decision about moving. That didn't mean I didn't miss having him around.

"I'll be there as soon as I can."

"Maverick?"

"Yeah?"

"Thank you. For everything," she whispered.

"See you soon, Lily," I told her as I hung up the phone and headed straight for Cotton's office.

Cotton and Guardrail were standing in his doorway talking when I walked up. They both turned their attention to me when I said, "I need to go to Tennessee for a few days."

"What's going on?" Cotton asked.

"I've just got some things I need to take care of. I won't be long," I clipped. I wasn't in the mood for a lecture tonight, and I knew I'd get one if Cotton knew that I was going to sign those adoption papers. He'd given me his blessing, but I knew he'd always hoped that I'd change my mind about it.

"And Henley?" Cotton inquired.

"Fuck," I mumbled. "I guess she'll have to go with me."

"Yeah, she will," Guardrail smirked, but I wasn't in the mood to debate with either of them. I ignored that fucking grin on his face as I headed for the door.

"She isn't going to be happy about it," I called out as I walked out into the hall.

I hadn't noticed that Guardrail followed me until he said, "I'll talk to her. You go get packed."

I didn't have time to argue, so I nodded and headed to my room to pack. As I threw my clothes into my duffle bag, my mind drifted to Henley. I wanted to think that having her there with me would make things easier, but I wasn't really sure how she'd feel about me signing those papers. Would she truly be able to understand why I was doing this? Could she come away from this without hating me? Fuck. How could I expect her to do something that I wasn't able to do myself?

Chapter 14

HENLEY

"**S**OMETHING'S COME UP, Henley. You're going to need to pack a bag," Guardrail ordered.

"Why? What's going on?" I asked, startled by his command.

"I don't have time to explain it all, but you'll be going to Tennessee with Maverick for a few days. He has some things to take care of, and since he is in charge of watching out for you, you'll have to go with him," he explained. "He's taking his cage to save time, so feel free to pack a suitcase."

"Really? Do I have to? I can't hang out here until he gets back?" I whined like a three-year-old child. I hated long road trips, and the thought of being confined in a car for hours upon hours with Maverick freaked me out. I couldn't even look at him without staring at those perfect full lips, thinking about that damn kiss.

"Like I said, I don't have time to explain all this shit to you, Henley. Just pack a bag and be ready to go within the hour."

"I'll be ready." I couldn't help but wonder if everything was alright. "Is Maverick okay? Is something wrong?"

"If he wants you to know, he'll tell you."

"Okay," I mumbled as I turned to leave.

"Henley, I don't know what you've done, but since you've been around, he's been better. Don't give up on him."

"I'll be ready in fifteen minutes," I told him. I went back to my room and started cramming my clothes into my suitcase. I couldn't stop thinking about what Guardrail said, and I wondered if it was really true. Was Maverick truly better because of something I'd done? I was lost in my own thoughts when Cassidy walked into my room.

"I just heard about Maverick. Road trip!"

I just grunted as I threw my make-up bag into my suitcase.

"Do you need any help packing?" she asked.

"No, I think I've got it," I told her as I continued to shove all my odds and ends into my suitcase.

Her eyebrows rose as she asked, "Are you okay with this?"

"Honestly? No. I'm totally freaking out," I confessed. "I have no idea what's going on, and …"

"It's going to be fine, Lee Bug. It's just for a few days, and you're going to love John Warren. He's absolutely precious. I wish I was going with you so I could see him, too. I've really missed him," she paused. She cleared her throat, trying to change the subject, as she said, "I've heard that Paris is a really neat place, and they have a beautiful lake."

"Why doesn't that make me feel any better?"

"You never know. You might just enjoy yourself." She smiled as she reached out and wrapped her arms around me, hugging me tightly. "Be yourself, and everyone will love you, including Maverick."

"Do you have any idea what's going on with him? Guardrail didn't tell me anything."

She released me from our embrace and looked me in the eye as she said, "No, but I have a feeling that this trip is going to be hard on him."

"Why does everyone keep saying that?"

"You weren't here to see him when he came back from taking John Warren to Lily and Goliath. It was hard to see him like that," she explained with tears filling her eyes.

"If going back there is going to be difficult for him, then having me there is only going to make it…" I started.

"No matter what is going on with him, having you there will only make it better. Now, stop worrying yourself to death about it and let's get a move on. If I know Maverick, he's already in the car ready to go."

"Alright. Let's do this," I told her as I grabbed the handle of my suitcase, tugging it out the door.

She was right. Maverick was already waiting for me at the end of the hall. He didn't say a word as I followed him out to the car. In fact, he didn't say anything for the first four hours of the drive. He just drove with his hands tightly gripping the steering wheel. The tension just rolled off of him, making it hard to know what I should do or say. I decided that this was one of those times that I just needed to sit there with my mouth shut. There was no need to poke the bear with a stick, so I just tried to keep my attention focused on the scenery outside my window. There were a couple of times that I noticed him looking over in my direction, but he never said a word. I wished he would say something. Anything. I had so many questions, but I couldn't work up the courage to ask him.

When I couldn't stand it any longer, I finally said, "I've got to go to the bathroom, and maybe get something to eat?"

"It's a long drive. We don't have time for a bunch of stops, Henley," he grumbled.

"I'm talking about five minutes, Maverick. I'll

make it quick. I promise," I pleaded.

Pulling off the interstate, he murmured something under his breath. As soon as he put the car in park, I got out and raced towards the front door of the convenience store.

"Five minutes!" I heard Maverick shout as the door shut behind me.

I was tempted to take my time, but I was afraid he wouldn't stop again if I didn't hurry. I finished in the restroom, bought a couple of drinks and a handful of snacks, and I quickly grabbed my bag of goodies, heading back to the car. Maverick was waiting outside for me when I walked out.

"I got us some snacks." I smiled, hoping to get some kind of reaction out of him.

"You planning on feeding an army with all that?"

"I wasn't sure how long it would be before we stopped again." He took a drink and a bag of chips from my hand as he started the car and pulled out onto the road.

Trying to make the best of the quiet time in the car, I used my phone to check my emails, send out a few text messages and finish reading my book. Every now and then, I would look over to check on Maverick, hoping that he might say something, tell me what was worrying him. But without fail, his attention was focused on the road, letting me know that he had no intention of talking to me. When the daunting silence got to be too much, I closed my eyes and fell asleep.

I had no idea how long I'd been asleep when I felt myself being carefully lifted out of the car. Without opening my eyes, I knew Maverick was cradling me in his arms. The warmth of his body was too inviting, and I was too damn exhausted to protest. So, I rested my head on his shoulder and let him carry me to the room.

I couldn't even remember him putting me in the bed, but I woke up the next morning with my head plastered on his bare chest. I slowly lifted myself up, trying my best not to wake him up and carefully eased myself onto the floor. I stopped at the edge of the bed, unable to keep my eyes from roaming over his chest, marveling at the beautiful artwork that marked his skin. It was the first time I'd seen the large tattoo across his broad chest, and my fingers twitched at my side, longing to reach out and touch him. My body yearned for him, overwhelming me with a desire like I'd never known before. I haven't had much experience with men… just one real boy-friend since high school. After I caught him cheating on me with my best friend, I'd sworn off guys altogether and tried to focus on my studies. Until now, I hadn't missed it. That spark, that desire to be with a man. I'd had my distractions with school and my family, and I was happy just being by myself. Now… it was different.

Now, I wanted *him*.

The white cotton sheet rested just below his hips, taunting me, begging me to crawl back into that bed next to him. My eyes slowly traveled up along the muscles of his chest, gradually stopping when I reached his handsome face. My heart ached as I looked at him sleeping so soundly, the burden that he carried with him every second of the day had seemed to melt away. Lying there with his face free from his dark thoughts, he actually looked peaceful, almost vulnerable. I wanted to curl up next to him and hold him close. I wanted to try to keep the demons from finding their way back to him.

"How long are you planning to stand there staring at me like that?" he grumbled with his eyes barely squinting open. Damn. The spell was broken.

"Well, you ruined it. For a minute there, you actually looked kind of *sweet*."

"Nothing about me is sweet, Slick," he smirked.

"Why don't you go back to sleep, and let me enjoy *Sweet Maverick* for a little while longer?" I teased, but he wasn't in the mood for it. "What time is it, Henley?" he demanded.

I looked over at the clock and told him, "8:30."

He closed his eyes and growled under his breath. For a second, I thought he was going to do like I suggested and sleep longer, but instead, he threw the covers back and sat at the edge of the bed. He dropped his head into his hands and rested his elbows on his knees, letting out a low, deep sigh.

"How much longer is the drive?" I asked apprehensively.

"We'll get there late tonight, but we need to get rolling," he said as he stood up and headed towards the bathroom. He stopped at the doorway and glanced back at me, lost in a thoughtful gaze. After a few seconds, he said, "I slept better last night than I have in months, even though you're like sleeping next to a damn heating pad. Hell, I'm surprised that I don't have third degree burns after lying next to you all night." I noticed just a glimmer of a smile creeping across his face before he closed the door behind him. Damn, I loved that smile… it's going to be the end of me.

I was already dressed and ready to go by the time Maverick had the car loaded. I knew he was in a rush, but I was in dire need of a cup of coffee. "So, how about some breakfast before we go?"

"Drive through," was all he said as he started the engine.

I'd already given up any hopes for pancakes and bacon, so I said, "Cool beans."

After we grabbed something to eat, it was several hours before we stopped again, and that was only to get more gas. The long drive was killing me. It would be different if Maverick would actually talk to me, but he just sat there stewing in his thoughts. I wanted to know what was going on in that head of his, but I was afraid I'd set him off. When I had finally worked up the courage, I asked him, "How'd you get the name Maverick?"

"Cotton."

"Okay… but why Maverick?" I pushed.

"He used to watch reruns of some old show called Maverick. He thought the guy reminded him of me," he said, looking over in my direction. "I've always stood up for what I believe in, even when it would be easier to just let things go."

"I like it. I think it suits you." I finally had him talking so I thought I would push a little further. "Are you going to tell me why we are going to Tennessee?"

"I have some papers to sign."

"Couldn't they just fax them to you or something?"

"No." One word. That's all I got, so I kept trying.

"Will I get to meet your brother while we're there?"

"Probably."

"Does he have a delightful personality like his brother?" I taunted. Surely one of them knew how to have a decent conversation.

He looked over to me with a smirk and said, "Of course."

That smile! I'd do just about anything to keep that smile on his face. I felt like I was getting somewhere, so I just kept talking. "Good to know. How about the others? Is this MC club like yours?"

"They're different," he clipped.

"How?" I prodded.

"Just different… safer, but a club nonetheless."

"By safer I'd assume that you mean they don't deal in illegal activities, so there are less threats to deal with?" When he didn't reply, I kept talking. "I guess that would make it easier. I mean not having to worry about who's waiting to take you down at every corner must have its advantages." The muscles in his throat began to twitch letting me know that it was time for me to redirect. "Cassidy says they have a lake there."

"Yeah, their club is just a few miles from the water."

"That would be so cool. I'd love to have a place where I could sit out on a big wide porch and drink my cup of coffee while I looked out over the water. Perfect way to start the day." Just the thought of a place like that made me wonder what I was going to do after college. After two more classes, I would be graduating, and I really had no idea what I was going to do. I'd always dreamed of being a graphic designer – creating images that could be seen all over the world. Now, I found myself wondering if Maverick would have a place in my life when this thing was all over. What did his future hold and would I be a part of it somehow? It was silly for me to even think about it. We barely knew each other. It was ridiculous, but a part of me liked the thought of having him in my life.

"If anyone could manage to get a place like that, it'd be you," Maverick said, pulling me from my thoughts.

I wondered about that remark. It seemed like a real compliment, but I didn't respond. Instead, I sat there in silence, looking out the window wishing we'd hurry up and pass the Tennessee state line. When the minutes rolled into an hour, I finally just closed my eyes and drifted off to sleep.

I woke up when Maverick nudged me with his elbow and said, "We're almost there. It's late, so we're just going to stay at the club tonight."

"Okay," I yawned with a deep breath, trying to pull myself awake. I was too tired to get nervous about meeting a bunch of new people, but I did have enough sense to know that I needed to brush out my hair and fix the mascara smudges from under my eyes. Just as I finished making myself look half-way presentable, he pulled through a small gate and stopped in front of the Devil Chaser's clubhouse. It was much smaller than Maverick's club, but even in the dark, I could tell that it was a really cool place. It had a rustic feel to it, and I couldn't wait to see what it looked like inside.

"Most of the guys aren't here, so it should be a pretty quiet night."

When I opened my car door and finally stood up and stretched wide, the muscles in my legs cried out in relief. "At this point, I don't care if Satan himself is in there. I'm just glad to be out of that damn car."

Chapter 15

MAVERICK

I WASN'T IN the mood to search for another hotel room, so I was relieved when Bishop gave me the okay to stay at the club tonight. He was already expecting me, but wasn't aware that Henley had come along. After asking a hundred damn questions, he finally agreed to let us both stay. I didn't blame him for being concerned. Bishop's the president of the club, and he'd worked hard to protect his brothers and their families. Having Henley with me made him apprehensive, but I assured him that we'd be gone as soon as I signed the adoption papers.

When I opened the door for Henley, I was surprised to see Courtney and Bobby sitting at the bar. I put my arm around Henley's waist, nudging her forward. I hadn't really had time to prepare her for Court, but I had a feeling that she could hold her own.

"Well, if it isn't *Mr. Serious* himself," Courtney called out as we walked over to them. "It's good to see you, stranger. Lily told us you were coming in tonight, but she didn't say that you were bringing your girlfriend."

"It's good to see you, Courtney. Been awhile. Have you been keeping yourself out of trouble?" I said laughing.

"Always!" she replied, trying to sound defensive. She motioned her head over in my direction and said, "He's a great guy. You know, once you get past all that broody moody stuff." She extended her hand out to Henley and said, "I'm Courtney, and this is my fiancé, Bobby."

Henley looked over to me, waiting for me to correct Courtney's girlfriend comment from earlier, and when I didn't, she said, "I'm Henley. It's nice to meet you both, and I'm glad to know that I'm not the only one that calls him out on his grim disposition."

"Tell me about it. It takes an act of Congress just to get the man to smile," Courtney laughed.

"Well, some things never change. Crack Nut, get your woman to behave," I teased. "Mind if I grab a beer?"

"Brother, it looks like you could use more than one. Grab us both a couple," he said smiling.

I reached in the cooler, grabbing us each a beer, and then sat down next to Bobby. "Bishop still around?"

"He had to go check on Tessa. She's had some trouble with the pregnancy, and they put her on bedrest for a couple of weeks. But before he left, he said for y'all to take one of the empty rooms. There's one down the hall. Second door on your right."

"Appreciate it," I told him, before Courtney started rambling on. She talked nonstop about school, the wedding, and *me*. She hadn't changed a bit since the last time I was here. When I had to lay low, the Devil Chasers opened their doors to me, on the condition that I helped them out with Courtney. They'd had some trouble with a rival MC gang that was trying to come into their territory, and they'd needed me to keep an eye on her. It gave me a chance to get to know them all, and I got to spend some extra time with John Warren. When everything went to hell back at home with Tony and his thugs, I had to return. Fortunately, things with the DC's were resolved shortly after I left.

Bobby and I listened to them carry on as we all drank several beers, and I was surprised that Henley never mentioned that we weren't a couple. Instead, she played along with the idea, letting them both think that she was mine. Even telling Courtney all about the pranks she'd pulled over the past few weeks, somehow making our relationship seem... *real*. They continued to talk and drink as Bobby told me about some of the new bikes they had been renovating, and how Gavin had been a great addition to their crew.

We'd been there talking for almost an hour, and we were all feeling the effects of the alcohol. It was good to see Courtney and Bobby again, and I was glad they were both doing so well. As Henley continued to talk, she nestled herself into the crook of my arm like it was something she had always done. Without thinking, I rested my hand on her hip and pulled her closer to me. It felt right having her there next to me, calming me, making me feel human for the first time in so long. She turned her head back to look at me, and when her eyes met mine, I couldn't stop myself from leaning down and pressing my lips against hers. The feel of her mouth against mine made the blood rush to my cock, instantly fueling my need to have her – all of her. She slowly turned her body facing me, pressing her hips against my growing bulge. I traced her bottom lip with my tongue, and when she opened up to me, I completely forgot that we weren't alone.

We were still locked in our embrace when Bobby announced, "I think that's our cue to head home, Court." He laughed as he stood up to leave, taking Courtney by the hand and leading her towards the door.

"I'll see you two love-birds tomorrow," Courtney shouted just before the door closed behind them.

Henley placed her hands on my chest, pulling herself away just long enough to say, "Where's our room?"

I didn't hesitate, didn't think about the consequences. I just took her hand and led her down the hall. As soon as I shut the door behind us, I said, "Are you sure about this?" I prayed that she hadn't changed her mind. I wanted her... *craved* her. Without me even realizing it, this woman had turned my world upside down and made me want... *more*.

"Absolutely," she said as she lifted herself up on her tiptoes and wrapped her arms around my neck, pulling me closer as she pressed her lips against mine. The kiss instantly became heated, intensifying my need for her. I took several steps forward until Henley's back was pressed against the wall. My hands slid down to her ass, lifting her off the ground as I grinded my throbbing cock against her. Her legs instinctively made their way around my waist, and the heat of her body set me on fire. An overwhelming need to extinguish the burn had me struggling to contain my craving for her. I'd never wanted anyone as much I as wanted her in that moment. My lips left her mouth, and slowly traveled down her long slender neck. Henley moaned with pleasure as her fingers raked through my hair and down the back of my neck. Her hips rocked against me, making my cock grow harder, prying against the zipper of my jeans.

"I've imagined having you like this, Henley. Your hot little body pressed against the wall while I fucked you," I whispered as her fingertips clawed at the back of my shirt, lifting it over my head. "You've thought about it, too. Haven't you? Feeling my cock inside you, fucking you until your body collapses around me?"

"Yes! Yes!" she cried out. "Please, Maverick." My mind flashed red at the sound of my road name coming from her lips. At any other time, it wouldn't have mattered. She'd called me Maverick a thousand times, but in that moment, something was different. I needed to hear her call me by my name.

"*Logan*," I corrected her. "Whenever we're alone, when I have my mouth on you," I whispered as I nipped at her neck. I reached down between her legs and pressed firmly against the fabric of her white shorts and whispered, "my fingers inside of you, or," a deep moan vibrated through her chest as I ground my cock against her, "when I'm fucking you senseless with my cock, I want to hear you crying out my name."

"Logan," she whimpered as the warmth of her breath swept across my neck. I'd never felt like this before. I'd never wanted something so much. She was more than I ever imagined, and it was impossible to resist her. I eased her shirt over her head, exposing her perfect round tits. I couldn't wait to get them in my mouth, feeling her squirm beneath me while I explored every inch of her body.

With her legs still wrapped around my waist, I carried her over to the edge of the bed. She lowered her feet to the floor, and slowly reached behind her back, removing her pink, lace bra. She didn't shy away from me when I watched her breasts fall free from the lace fabric, taunting me, begging for my mouth. She was absolutely stunning, but I wanted to see more of her – all of her.

"I want to see *all of you*, Henley." She eagerly released the buttons of her shorts and let them drop to the floor. With her eyes locked on mine, she stepped out of them, leaving her sandals behind. She stood before me wearing only a pink pair of lacy panties. Fuck me… she was gorgeous.

"*All of it*, Henley."

Her fingers trailed along her hips as she lowered them, inch by inch, down her long legs, her eyes never leaving mine as she teased me. She gently kicked them to the side and faced me, waiting to see my reaction. I was pleased that she wasn't intimidated by my intense stare, letting my eyes slowly roam over every inch of her. Instead, she seemed to relish the fact that her body was affecting me to such a degree. Her head cocked to the side, and her eyes drifted to the tent in my jeans. With her hands now on her hips, a wicked smile crept across her face.

"Your turn, *Logan*. I want to see *all of you*," she said playfully, using my own words against me.

It was difficult to restrain myself with her standing there looking so fucking tempting, but I took my time, watching her reaction as I slowly undressed. I needed to know that she wanted this, and watching her squirm in front of me, left me with no doubt. Her eyes widened with anticipation as I gradually lowered my zipper, taking my time to ease my jeans down my hips. Her teeth toyed with her bottom lip as I tossed my clothes to the side. A light whimper echoed through the room when she noticed my hard cock beneath my boxers.

"All of it," she demanded softly.

Without hesitation, I tugged them off and tossed them across the room. She stood there motionless while she looked at me… her eyes filled with lust as she watched my hand reach for my cock. I took my dick in my hand and squeezed, relieving some of the throbbing pressure. I felt it pulse against my hand as I slowly stroked it, groaning out a curse. Henley bit her lip harder as she watched me, her eyes focused totally on the motion of my hand. I just knew she was wet for me, wanting to feel my cock inside her.

I stepped closer, and put my free hand on her

ass, pulling her body against mine and whispered, "Do you like what you see, Henley? Are you wet for me?" I didn't wait for her to answer as my hand slid between her legs. My fingers brushed against her entrance, and I found my answer. "Yeah, you're wet for me. You want my cock deep inside you, making you cum, but you're going to have to wait for my cock, baby." I pressed my lips against hers as I lowered her down to the bed. The warmth of her naked body enveloped me, and I wondered how much more I could take before I was inside her.

My need for her was building, burning deep inside my gut. Fuck. I wanted to take my time with her, but seeing her body respond to my touch was driving me crazy. I continued to lick and suck along the lines of her neck and shoulder, slowly trailing down to her breasts while her whimpers and groans urged me on. I took one in the palm of my hand, gently squeezing as my tongue twirled around her nipple. Her hips bucked against me as I teased her with my mouth.

"Soon, Henley," I groaned, kissing my way down her flat stomach. My hands slid under her ass, pulling her closer to my mouth. I thought she was going to jump out of her skin when I pressed the flat of my tongue against her clit. Her fingers dove into my hair, guiding me as her knees opened wider. I teased her with my mouth, bringing her close to the edge, but pulling away before she could orgasm. The taste of her against my tongue was driving me wild. I had to hear her cum. I couldn't wait to feel her pussy tighten around my cock. Slipping two fingers deep inside, I began to fuck her with my hand. Her hips rocked against me, grinding hard against my fingers while she tried to get the friction she needed to find her orgasm. I wanted to be inside of her when she broke, I pulled back, making her wait for it. She groaned in frustration when I found her g-spot, teasing her even as I curled my fingers against it.

She was writhing beneath me, tortured by her overwhelming need to find release. I couldn't take it anymore. I had to be inside her. I lifted myself up between her legs and reached for a condom. A small smile of relief washed over her face when she watch me roll the latex down my cock.

"Hurry," she grumbled as she wrapped her legs around my waist, pulling me closer to her entrance. I looked down at her, captivated by her lust filled eyes.

I brushed my cock against her clit, and demanded, "Tell me… tell me you want this."

"Umm…hmm," she murmured.

"I need to hear the words, Henley. Tell me."

Her eyes locked on mine, and I knew her answer before she even said it. "I want you, Logan.

I want all of you," she whispered, her voice low and raspy. She wound her arms around my neck, and I felt her quiver beneath me as I thrusted deep inside her. Her hands pushed against my chest letting me know she needed time to adjust. After a few seconds, her hips slowly began to roll against mine, urging me inside her. Not wanting to hurt her, I slowly began to move, but kept a slow, steady rhythm.

"More," she pleaded.

Her body grew rigid as I began to thrust deeper, harder. Her snug pussy throbbed against my cock, weakening all of my restraint. I intended to go slow… needed to go slow, but I couldn't fucking stop. Her pussy was so tight, so ready. I couldn't restrain myself any longer. She was more than I had ever expected, making me lose all my sense of control. Her nails dug into my lower back as her hips bucked against mine, meeting my every thrust with more force… more intensity. I could feel the pressure building in my cock as her walls constricted against me.

Her head reared back as she shouted, "Oh god, Logan!"

"Fuck," I groaned as her pussy tightened, clenching down against me. She panted wildly, moaning and clawing at my back when I increased my pace. I knew she was close to the edge, unable to stop the inevitable torment of her building orgasm. The muscles in her body grew taut, and her body stilled as her release took over. I continued to drive into her, the sounds of my body pounding against hers echoing throughout the room. My hands reached under her, lifting her ass off of the bed, and continued to thrust harder and deeper, until I finally came inside her.

Her body fell limp under me. I remained still, seated deep inside her, not ready for this to end. I rested my head on her chest and listened to her rapid heartbeat begin to steady. Her breathing began to slow to the point that I thought she had actually fallen asleep. I looked up at her and was surprised to see a sexy smile on her face. I settled myself beside her, and she slowly began to wiggle her way into the crook of my arm and laid her head down on my chest.

With her fingers tracing the lines of my tattoo, she said, "It was nice to see you have a good time tonight."

"Yeah, it's been awhile," I told her.

When she looked up at me, I saw something in her eyes that I wasn't prepared to see. God. I hoped I wasn't right. I was the last man a woman like her needed to fall for. My life was a fucking mess. I should've protected her from my darkness, not pulled her into it. Fuck. I was a selfish bastard. I knew I should say something, warn her somehow, but feeling her body pressed against mine felt too fucking good. I couldn't let her go, not yet. We laid tangled in each other's arms until we finally fell asleep.

I woke up early, the dread of the day ahead of me already creeping in, making my chest so tight that it was difficult to breathe. When I looked down and found Henley still draped across my chest, I felt an instant sense of calm wash over me. I could've spent the entire day wrapped in her arms, but I knew Lily was waiting for me. I gave her a light kiss on her forehead and tried to pull myself from her arms without waking her. It took some effort, but I finally managed to wedge myself free and headed for the bathroom.

After a hot shower, I got dressed and sat on the edge of the bed. Henley hadn't budged since I had gotten out of the bed. Leaning down close to her ear, I whispered, "Hey, Slick. Wake up."

She groaned as she threw her arm over her eyes, trying to block out the light. "What time is it?" she fussed.

"It's early, go back to sleep," I told her as I stood up and kissed her on the forehead.

"Are you leaving?" she asked as she lifted her arm, peaking up at me.

"Yeah, but I won't be gone long."

"I hope it goes okay," she whispered.

"It will, now go back to sleep," I told her as I headed out the door.

Just like I thought, Bobby was working on his computer in his office. I stuck my head inside his doorway and said, "Hey, man. I've got to run over to Lily's for a bit. Mind keeping an eye on Henley for an hour or so? She's still in bed."

"Sure. Not a problem. You want me to bring her over there when she gets up?" he offered.

"That'd be great. Just give me a call before you leave. I'm not sure how long it will take."

"You got it. Courtney is in the kitchen with Taylor making cookies for the kids. I'm sure they can keep her entertained while you're gone," he laughed.

I sent a text to Lily that I was on my way, and when I pulled into the driveway, she was waiting for me on the front porch. She had John Warren propped up on her hip next to her full, obviously very pregnant belly. Looking at her, holding her family close to her heart, gave me a sense of peace. John Warren had his family. Seeing him for the first time in months, I was surprised by how much he had changed. He watched me apprehensively as I made my way up to the porch.

"Hey, Lily." He looked up at her, waiting to see what her reaction would be. I was a stranger to him, and he wasn't quite sure what to make of me yet.

When she leaned in and gave me a hug, he piped up and said, "Bye-bye."

"He isn't going anywhere yet silly. This is Maverick. I've told you all about him," Lily explained.

"Momma," he said as he grasped Lily's arm tightly.

"Hey there, little man. You've grown a foot since the last time I saw you." John Warren studied me, almost like he was trying to decide if he knew me, or if he even wanted to know me.

"Our appointment is in fifteen minutes. We better get rolling if we want to be on time," Lily started. "You wanna just ride with us?"

"Sure," I told her as I grabbed the diaper bag off of the rocking chair. Once she had John Warren buckled into his car seat, she said, "The place is just down on the square, and they said it wouldn't take long. The nurse said that they'd just run a cotton swab inside your cheek and then John Warren's. When the results come back, we can sign off on the papers."

Her voice cracked when she spoke. I knew she was worried that I might change my mind, decide that I didn't want them to adopt my son, but there was no chance of that. It was impossible to miss the way he looked at her, like a son looks at his mother, and I would never take that away from him.

"Sounds good."

"I really appreciate you coming all the way here. I know…" she started.

"It's fine, Lily. I know you're eager to get this thing done," I clipped.

"Maverick, he's happy. He really is. We'll give him…"

"Lily, stop…. I know he is happy. Anybody can see that, and I know you'll give him the life he deserves. That's why I brought him to you in the first place, and I'm not about to change my mind now." My chest tightened at the thought. There was no turning back after this. I had to wonder what the hell was wrong with me. I should've had some doubts, some second thoughts, but I didn't. When I looked at John Warren, I still found myself questioning how all of this happened.

On the way to the hospital, Lily talked non-stop about everything that had happened since I'd been gone. Once we got there, the test didn't take long, and they said that we should have the results later today or in the morning. Usually these kinds of tests take days, even weeks, to come back, but Sheppard's wife, Ana, worked at the local hospital. She called in a few favors and was able to get a rush put on it.

As soon as we were done, I texted Bobby to let him know that we were heading back to the house. By the time we got back to Lily's, Bobby's SUV was already in the driveway. When we walked in, I was relieved to catch the smell of coffee coming from the kitchen. Goliath was pouring himself a cup when I walked in.

"Mind if I grab one of those?" I asked without even saying hello.

"There's a fresh pot brewing... help yourself," Goliath told me as he motioned his hand over toward the coffee pot.

I was pouring myself a cup when Henley walked over to Lily and said, "You must be Lily. I'm Henley, a friend of Maverick's."

Shaking her hand, Lily replied, "It's great to finally meet you, Henley. I'm glad Maverick had you to tag along, so he didn't have to make that long drive alone."

"I don't think he really even knew I was there. He's a man of few words," Henley laughed. She gently ran her hand over John Warren's head and said, "He is just too cute for his own good."

"He's going to be a lady killer, that's for sure," Courtney chimed in.

When I looked over to Henley, she caught my eye for just a moment, then looked away. She twirled a loose strand of her hair around her finger as she listened to the conversation floating around the room. This wasn't the Henley I knew. She wasn't her normal confident self. The doubts of last night were rolling around in her head. I knew I should go over to her, try to ease the awkwardness that was building between us, but I couldn't make myself take that first step. She was right to have her doubts. She should fucking regret it. She was innocent and pure, and the last thing she needed was to get involved with a man like me – a man tarnished by his past.

Chapter 16

HENLEY

W HAT THE HELL is wrong with me? I can't even look at him. It's stupid. I know I have no reason to feel like this. I know last night didn't mean anything or did it? He's not acting all weird. At least, I don't think he is. So why I am feeling so off center?

"I was going to take Henley into town and show her the shops around the square. Do you want to go with us?" Courtney asked Lily.

Lily looked over to Goliath and asked, "Can you keep an eye on JW for me? I don't think it's a good idea to take him with us. You know how he likes to get his hands into stuff."

"No problem. I'll take him over to the clubhouse with us. You can just meet us over there when you're done," he answered, looking at her like she was the most precious thing in the world. This huge brute of a man was wrapped tight around her little finger, and he didn't seem to mind that everyone knew it. I liked that about him.

"Cool beans. Let's roll, chickadees," Courtney said as she motioned for us to follow her out the door.

I looked over to Maverick once more, hoping that he might do or say something to settle my nerves, but he was still busy talking to Bobby. He didn't even seem to notice when I walked passed him, heading out the door. Damn.

The minute we got in the car, Courtney started her inquisition. "Sooo… what's the deal with you and Maverick?"

"Courtney," Lily scolded. "At least give us time to get a cup of coffee before you start laying into her." They both laughed, but I didn't miss that sparkle in Courtney's eye. There was no way she was going to leave it alone.

"Oh come on, Lily. You know you're just as curious as I am about what's going on with the two of them," Courtney laughed.

"I'd tell you if I knew, but to be honest… I don't know what the hell is going on," I confessed as I dropped my head into my hands.

"I don't imagine Maverick would make it easy. Why don't you just start from the beginning, and we'll help you sort it all out," Courtney offered.

"That's just it. I don't know where to start. I never intended to fall for him, and …" I started, but stopped myself when I realized what I was saying.

"You know, no one would blame you for falling in love with Maverick, Henley," Lily assured me. "He's a really good guy. He's been through a lot, and it would be good to see him with someone who can make him happy."

"And he's easy on the eyes," Courtney chimed in, and we all laughed.

"He's just so…"

"Frustrating?" Courtney asked. "Hard headed? A pain in the ass?"

"Yep! All of the above."

"All men are, but when you get past that… past all the stuff that doesn't really matter, then you'll find the real man hidden beneath. That will be the man you will come to love, and the other stuff doesn't really matter anymore," Lily explained.

"In other words, you have to get past all the bullshit to find the pot of gold at the end of the rainbow," Courtney snickered.

They continued their line of questioning all the way downtown. Paris was a small town, but it had a lot of personality. The town square had several specialty shops and boutiques, and I was looking forward to going into all of them. When we stopped at the first store, Maverick's car pulled in right next to us. Without giving his presence a second thought, the girls got out of the car and headed inside. I, on the other hand, was shocked to see him there. I sat there staring at him like he had lost his mind. When I didn't move, Maverick gave me a sexy smirk and motioned with his hand for me to follow the girls inside the store. I don't know why I was so surprised that he was there. Since the day I walked into the club, he always made sure that I was safe. I quickly realized that Courtney was right… *I just had to get past all the bullshit.*

Courtney never stopped talking while we walked around all the quaint little shops, telling me every story that popped into her head. I've never laughed so much in my entire life. I loved getting to know them both, and I could have spent the entire day looking around at all the different stores. Unfortunately, Lily was getting tired. Although she never complained, her face was growing pale, and I could tell that she was wearing down.

"You ready to head back?" I asked.

"Do you mind? I really need to get back and feed John Warren," she explained.

"Sure… ready whenever you are," I told her.

After Courtney finished checking out, she grabbed her bags, and we headed back to the car. With Maverick following close behind, we drove back to the clubhouse. When we got there, the guys were gathered in the kitchen talking about what they were going to fix for dinner. Without saying a word, Maverick sat down at the table beside John Warren and began feeding him a handful of Cheerios. Goliath and one of his brothers pulled out several steaks from the refrigerator and started getting them ready for the grill.

"You got one of those for me, Shep?" Courtney asked as she peered over his shoulder and watched him sprinkle the seasoning on the steaks.

"You know it. We've got plenty. Hope y'all are hungry," Sheppard told her. With his blonde hair and blue eyes, I thought he looked more like a model than a biker. There was a warmth to his smile that gave him a wholesomeness that I wouldn't have expected from one of the Devil Chasers.

"Yes, we're starving… well, I am, but I'm always hungry these days," Lily told him as she patted her round stomach. "Have you heard anything from Ana?"

"Nothing yet. She checked the lab before she left, and they weren't ready yet," Sheppard told her.

Goliath walked over to her with his eyebrows furrowed with concern and gave her a light kiss on her forehead. "She'll have them in the morning. Now, why don't you go rest for a bit while we get dinner ready? You look exhausted."

"Okay. I could use a little break. Just call me

when it's ready," she told him. Before she turned to leave, she reached up and kissed him on the lips.

I felt a twinge of jealousy as I watched them together. They had it all… they were a family and John Warren was the one that brought them together. I wondered if Maverick felt the same way. Did it hurt him to see them together, to see the family that he didn't have?

I leaned over to him and said, "Hey."

"Hey. How did things go today?" he asked.

"I had a great time, but I'm sure you already knew that, since you were there the whole time," I answered.

"Just keeping an eye on things," he said, sounding almost defensive.

"You should've spent some time with John Warren or Gavin. You didn't have to spend the day watching over me. It's not like anyone would follow us all the way to Tennessee."

"Not taking any chances," he said as he handed John Warren his sippy cup. I'll admit it. I liked that, even with everything that was going on in his life, he was still there looking out for me.

"So… did everything go okay this morning?" I was almost afraid to ask. Lily told me about the DNA test, and I wasn't sure how he'd feel about me knowing.

"Not much to it," he mumbled. His shoulders grew tense, obviously not wanting to talk about it.

"Okay. Well, I guess I'll go call Cassidy and check in. I know she'll be worried. I'll be back in time for dinner."

"Take your time. It's going to take them awhile to get dinner ready," he explained.

When I got up from the table, a part of me wished he had asked me to stay. I wanted him to talk to me about what was going on in his head, but he still wasn't ready to let me in. I wondered if I would ever be able to get through that wall he'd put up. It scared me to think that I might never get past it.

On the way to get my phone, I heard a huge ruckus coming from one of the bedrooms. I couldn't really tell what was going on, but someone was obviously upset. Curiosity got the best of me, so I peeked my head inside the doorway and found three men sitting on a sofa, shouting curses at the television screen. They each had a video game controller in their hand, and the sounds of gunfire exploded around the room.

One of them jumped up and shouted, "Come on, Levi! Don't go out in the open like that. That's a dumbass move!"

"Shut the fuck up, man. I got this," he said, defending himself. None of them seemed to notice when I stepped into the room.

They continued to shout back and forth

while each of them tried to defeat their opponent. The game was really heating up when one of their phones chimed with a text message. The man looked down at his phone and said, "I gotta run."

"What the hell, Conner? We're in the middle of a death match."

"Duty calls. We'll get 'em next time," he told him as he tossed his controller down on the sofa and headed for the door. When he finally noticed me standing there, his eyes roamed up and down my body. With his eyebrow arched high, he gave me a mischievous grin. I rolled my eyes and walked past him, heading for the sofa.

"Mind if I play?" I asked them, walking over and picking up the controller.

Without even asking who I was or what I was doing there, one of them asked, "You know how to play?" The minute he looked at me, I knew he was Gavin. I'd know those eyes anywhere. His hair was lighter and he wasn't as filled out as Maverick, but there was no doubt that he was Maverick's brother.

"Yeah… I've played a time or two," I said confidently, sitting down beside him.

"Well, let's see what you've got, sweet thang," Gavin smirked as his focus returned to the game.

It had been awhile since I had played, but I managed to hold my own. Before long, we were all shouting and screaming at each other like we'd been playing together for years. We tried our best to take down the enemy, and I was doing really well. Every time I got a good shot, Gavin and Levi would both cheer me on. I was having a blast. My kills were really adding up, and I'd only died twice, when I felt Maverick's presence enter the room.

None of us even acknowledged that he had walked up, there was no time. We were all too engrossed in the game to even speak to him. After a few minutes, with his eyes still trained on the TV, Gavin said, "Good to see you, man. Your friend here is an amazing shot."

"Is that right?" Maverick asked, looking over to me smiling.

"Yep," Gavin said. He nudged me with his elbow and continued, "I might have just found the perfect woman. She's beautiful and knows how to quick scope a sniper rifle."

The second the words left Gavin's mouth, Maverick's smile vanished. "Dinner's ready," he snapped, sounding almost pissed.

"Just a second… I've almost got him," I shouted with my eyes still glued to the screen. When the last guy dropped to the ground, Gavin and Levi reached out and gave me a high five.

"Did you see that? We just beat our high score," Gavin said proudly.

"Conner is going to be pissed that he missed

that!" Levi said laughing.

As soon as my feet hit the floor, Maverick took hold of my hand and led me out into the hall, closing the door behind us. Before I had a chance to ask him if something was wrong, my back was against the wall, and he was kissing me. It was no gentle kiss. There was nothing soft or sweet about it. It was demanding and intense, and I loved every minute of it. His body ground against mine, and we were both lost in the heat of the moment when Gavin stepped out in the hall. Maverick pulled back, releasing me from our embrace and growled. Yes… *growled* – like a mad dog hovering over his precious bone.

Gavin sighed and said, "Well, *damn*. I thought I'd found the one." He winked at me as he patted Maverick on the shoulder. "Let's go, big brother. Dinner is getting cold."

Chapter 17

MAVERICK

WHEN I SAW Gavin looking at Henley like she was the star on top of the fucking Christmas tree, I lost it. Enough said.

"Are you going to tell me what that was all about?" Henley whispered as we walked down the hall towards the kitchen.

"No."

"Really? You're not going to say ..." she started.

"No," I told her firmly.

"Alrighty then," she said sarcastically. "Just so you know, I think Gavin is really nice, and it was fun hanging out with him."

"Good to know."

"I'm sure you've missed him. I mean... it has to be hard being so far away from him, but I can tell he's happy here. The guys seem to like him."

I didn't respond. There was nothing to say. Yes, I missed my brother, and yes, he seemed to be doing great here. It was a good move for him to prospect here, but I had no intention of talking about it. I had other things on my mind.

After dinner, everyone went their separate ways. Henley helped the girls finish cleaning up the kitchen and then, headed back to the room. I hadn't had much time to talk to Gavin alone, so I went to the bar to have a few beers with him.

"Things seem to be going pretty well for you," I told him.

"Yeah, it's been good, really good. The guys are great, and I love working in the garage. You should see some of the bikes and cars they pull through here. They've really made a name for themselves," he explained. His eyes gleamed with pride while he talked about his work in the garage, and it meant a lot to me. When mom died, we both took it hard, but it was different for Gavin. He was just a kid and still needed his mother's guidance. I tried to be there for him, but he was just too young and naïve. He had to figure things out for himself. I always thought he'd just follow in my footsteps and join Satan's Fury, but seeing him now… I knew he'd made the right decision. He'd found his way, and he'd done it on his own.

"I'm glad you're a part of it. It's good to see you happy."

"What about you?" he asked hesitantly. "Are you sure about signing off on the adoption tomorrow?"

"Yeah. I'm sure."

"You know, I'd understand if you were having second thoughts or something, but John Warren…"

"I'm not having any doubts, Gavin. I know he's where he needs to be," I clipped.

"You're right. I know that, now. I've never told you this, but back then, I thought you were wrong. I thought it was a shitty thing for you to give him up. I really did, but when I saw him here with *them*, I understood. I understood why you did it. You did the right thing."

As soon as those words came out of his mouth something shifted inside of me. Just knowing that he actually got why I did it, made the weight I had been carrying around seem lighter.

"Thanks for telling me that, Gavin. It means a lot."

"So what's the story with the girl?" he prodded.

"Nothing to tell. I'm keeping an eye on her until we find the guys that killed Skidrow. End of story."

"Nah. There's more to it than that, and you know it. I saw the way you were looking at her, *and* the way you had her pinned against the wall. She means something to you."

"Maybe so, but it doesn't matter."

"It matters. Everybody needs someone that they can care about Maverick, even *you*," he told me as he took a drink of his beer.

It was after three in the morning by the time Gavin and I left the bar. I figured that Henley would be pissed that I was coming in so late, but when I crawled into bed, she didn't hesitate curling up next to me. With her head resting on my shoulder and her arm draped across my chest, she whispered, "Everything okay?"

"It is now," I told her as I kissed her on top of her head. "It's late, go back to sleep."

The alcohol was clouding my thoughts, making it difficult to think straight, but I'm almost certain that she said, "In case you were wondering… I wasn't interested in Gavin or anyone else, for that matter. I only want you… just you."

The room was silent. I could feel the rise and fall of her chest as her breathing became slow and deep. Even though she was sleeping soundly, her words continued to echo through my mind, and I wondered if I had imagined her saying those words to me.

"Henley?" I whispered, but she didn't answer. The room was spinning, so I finally gave in to my intoxicated state, and fell asleep. I couldn't have been out for more than a few hours, when I heard someone pounding on the door.

"Maverick!" Goliath shouted as he continued to slam his fist into my door. It felt like I had barely closed my eyes when he said, "It's time to roll, man. Ana just called and the test is back."

Why the fuck did I drink so much? My head was throbbing, and the light creeping in through the window was only making it worse. "Just a minute!" I shouted back. Henley was nowhere in sight when I pulled myself out of bed.

Wearing only a pair of boxers, I opened the door and asked, "Have you seen Henley?"

"She's out front with Lily. She can hang out here with Bobby or…"

"No, she's going with us," I told him. "Just give me five minutes." I still reeked of alcohol, and I needed a hot shower to clear my head. Goliath nodded as I closed the door behind him.

I turned the hot water on high and stepped into the shower, trying to wash away the fog of my hangover. It didn't help. My head was still pounding while I got dressed and headed down the hallway. When I opened the back door, the heat of the early morning sun hit me like a brick wall. I still hadn't gotten used to the Tennessee humidity, and I could already feel the sweat begin to trickle down my back. Henley walked over to me with a bottle of cold water and a couple of aspirin in her hand. "I thought you could use this."

"Thanks, Slick," I told her, taking the bottle from her hand. Her full lips curved into a sexy smile, tempting me to pull her close. "You ready to go?"

She laid the palm of her hand on my chest and said, "You really want me to go? I don't mind staying here. I can hang out with Bobby or Gavin until you get back."

"No, you're coming. Lily said it shouldn't take long, so I thought I'd show you around the lake when we got done, maybe grab a bite to eat."

"I'd like that."

With Lily and Goliath following behind us in their car, we headed over to the lawyer's office. We drove in silence, both of us lost in our own thoughts. I couldn't stop thinking about the night that I took JW back to Lily and Goliath – the night that sealed my fate, our fate. Every decision I'd made over the past year had a rippling effect, and I wondered if it all ended today. Would it – could it ever *really* end?

When we pulled into the parking lot, Ana was leaning against her car with a large yellow envelope in her hand. Her hair was pulled up in a ponytail, and she was wearing her doctor scrubs. Even in her work clothes, it was easy to see why Sheppard had fallen for her. She was beautiful and smart. Almost dying in that river was the best thing that ever happened to him.

Goliath pulled in next to me, and as we were getting out of the car, Ana walked over to us with a troubled look on her face. When she reached Lily, she said, "Hey, I need to talk to you before we go inside."

"Why? What's going on?" she asked.

The distressed look on Ana's face said it all. Something was wrong.

"It's the DNA test results. I don't know how to tell you this…" she started as her eyes skirted over to me. Fuck. What the hell was that look? Whatever was bothering her obviously had something to do with me, but I had no idea what it could be.

"What is it? Just say it, already," I demanded, feeling my heart pound against my chest. I tried to think of all the things that they might find in a DNA test. Was John Warren sick? Did he have some kind of genetic defect because of me?

Lily looked at Ana with a pleading look in her eyes. "Just tell us Ana," she begged.

"The test results showed that …. Maverick isn't John Warren's father. After analyzing all the markers, they determined that the percentages were just too low for him to be the father," she explained.

"Then, the fucking test is wrong!" I roared.

"I don't know what to say. There has to be some kind of mistake! We all know that Maverick is John Warren's father!" Lily shouted hysterically. "It just doesn't make any sense!"

A million thoughts were running through my head, and when I tried to speak, the words just wouldn't come. The rage began to boil in my gut when I finally realized what Ana's words really meant.

"Lily, I don't know what to say. I've gone over it hundred times. The results show that Maverick is indeed a close relative, but he's not the father," she tried to explain.

As soon as the word relative came from her mouth, I knew. Gavin is John Warren's father. I think a part of me had known all along that I wasn't his father. I'd felt it whenever I held him in my arms, certain something wasn't right. Now, hearing the words out loud… knowing that I hadn't been fucking crazy, made the ground shake beneath me. How the hell could I have been so goddamn blind? I took a deep breath trying to slow the storm of thoughts that were spinning in my head. I couldn't figure out how the fuck this happened? *Gavin*… Gavin was John Warren's *father*. I was sure of it. Fuck! How could he watch me go through hell, and never say a goddamn thing?

Fury soared through my body. I'd spent the past six months thinking I was some kind of monster. Gavin knew how tormented I was, how broken I had become and the self-loathing I felt for not being the father that John Warren need-ed. I thought I was incapable of being there for him… *my own* child. I detested the very thought of it. I tried to make excuses, telling myself that I was protecting him from the club. But, I knew that was really never it. It was me, only me I was protecting him from.

"Maverick," Henley whispered with a pained look on her face. She placed her hand on my arm, pulling me from my thoughts.

"It's Gavin. He's the father. He's the only living *relative* I have," I told Lily through gritted teeth. I took another deep breath, trying to calm my anger. I'd never felt such rage, such hurt. I took a step back, taking a deep breath. Then, just as suddenly as the onslaught of my initial rage from Gavin's betrayal, it happened. Like a dim light shining through the black clouds, the darkness that had been surrounding me for fucking months was starting to fade away as an overwhelming sense of relief washed over me. Like the rolling in of the ocean's tide, wave after wave of increasing relief, cleaning me of my guilt, my self-hatred and my despair. John Warren wasn't my son. I wasn't crazy. I wasn't losing my mind. My instincts were right all along. "Call him. He won't do anything to stand in your way of the adoption. He knows JW belongs with you," I told her.

"But how? How did this happen?" Lily asked with her voice trembling.

"He failed to mention that he was screwing Hailey, so you'll have to ask him about that," I snapped. The very thought of him being with

Hailey and never telling me about it, made my hands tremble with anger.

"I'll call him," Goliath told her as he wrapped his arms around her, holding her close to his chest. "We'll figure this thing out."

I couldn't take it anymore. I had to get the hell out of there. I needed to get this shit sorted in my head before I talked to Gavin. Right now, I couldn't think about it. I needed an escape.

"I'm taking Henley over to Paris Landing. Call me if you need me," I told them, taking hold of Henley's hand, and without either of us saying goodbye, I led her over to the car. I knew it was a shitty thing to do, leaving them alone to sort out this mess with Gavin, but I couldn't stay. I wasn't ready to deal with my brother.

I started the engine and neither of us spoke as I pulled out of the parking lot. I'd been driving for almost an hour when Henley cleared her throat and asked, "Hey… are you okay?"

"No, but I will be," I told her.

"Maverick, I'm really sorry," she told me.

"Nothing for you to be sorry about, Henley. This had nothing to do with you."

"Maybe not, but I'm still sorry all the same." She tried to brush her long bangs behind her ear and looked out the window. She let out a deep sigh before she said, "I'm just going to say it. I'm pissed at Gavin. Totally, absolutely pissed! Like chop off his balls kind of pissed. He's such an asshole for not telling you," she snapped. "I know it wouldn't have been easy, but he should have said something! Like, '*Hey, Maverick, I screwed your girlfriend. Sorry about that!*'"

"He saw the hell I was going through. How could he not say something?" I asked.

"I don't know. I can't imagine keeping something like that from Cassidy, but I'm sure Gavin had his reasons."

"I don't give a fuck what his reasons were, he should've talked to me about it."

"You're right. So what now?" she asked.

"I don't know. I just don't know."

"You'll sort it out. He's your brother, and he's about to find out that he's a father. It isn't going to be easy for him."

"You know what's crazy? I'm actually *relieved* that Gavin's the father. Totally, profoundly… relieved. How fucked up is that?" I confessed. "Don't get me wrong. I *love* John Warren, always have. But when I held him in my arms, it just didn't feel like he was *mine*. It's hard to explain. Something didn't feel right. I cared for him. Loved him and wanted to protect him, but I felt this emptiness in the pit of my stomach. I thought I was fucked up, that something was wrong with me, and I honestly felt like he was better off with Lily and Goliath."

"There was never anything wrong with you, Maverick. Your instincts were right, and in the end, you were doing what you thought was best for John Warren. That's all that really matters."

"I really did want him to be happy, to be safe. I knew Lily would be a good mother to him," I told her.

"Of course, you did. Lily and Goliath adore that child. You made them all very happy."

"Gavin…" I started, but his name got stuck in my throat.

"Is an *asshole*," she said, laughing under her breath.

When I looked over to her and saw that sexy, little grin spreading across her face, I couldn't help but smile back at her. Damn. My world had just been turned upside down, and Henley was here making me fucking smile. What was it about this girl? She had me thinking I might just have a future worth fighting for – a future with her.

Chapter 18

HENLEY

T HE MINUTE MAVERICK parked the car, I jumped out and headed for the dock. It was such a beautiful day, and I wanted to get a better view of all the boats. As I walked along the wooded walkway, the warmth of the afternoon sun was comforting. The waves rocked back and forth beneath my feet, and the cool water seemed to call out my name, begging me to jump in. I continued to walk along the narrow wooded path, completely enthralled with the luxury house boats that lined the dock, and I desperately wanted to look inside one of them. A large, white yacht with a golden trim caught my attention, and I just had to look inside. Leaning over to peek in one of the windows, I heard Maverick's footsteps coming up behind me. When I looked over at him, there was a mischievous gleam in his eyes. He grabbed my hand and started pulling me towards the back of the yacht.

"Whoa! What are you doing?" I asked as my feet stumbled behind him.

"Watch your step," he warned, stepping over the ledge and onto the massive boat.

As I followed him up on the railing, I read the name, *The Emma Lou* that was written on the side. I'd never heard him talk about anyone named Emma, so I asked, "Wait… do you actually know the people who own this boat?"

"No," he answered nonchalantly. Still holding my hand, he gently tugged me towards the back door of the boat.

"What do you mean, *no*? Doesn't that mean we're trespassing?" I questioned. I quickly looked around to see if anyone was watching us. I'd never done anything like this, and I couldn't imagine being any more excited than I was at that moment.

"Technically, yes," he laughed. He reached for his wallet and pulled out one of his credit cards, carefully nudging it between the door and the lock. When the door popped open, he gave me a devilish grin and motioned for me to step inside.

"What if someone saw us?" I asked, looking out the large, glass window still paranoid that someone might have seen us.

"Then, we'll probably get arrested," he snickered.

"Maverick!"

"Henley, look around. No one has been on this boat in weeks. There are no swimsuits, no food or drinks. Besides, it's not like we're going to steal their boat. We're just looking around," he explained as he leaned against the kitchen sink.

"I've never been on one of these before. Have you?" I asked, running my hand over the smooth marble countertop.

"First time," he said, following me into the living room.

When I looked around, I was amazed at how luxurious the yacht really was. Every corner and crevice sparkled with elegance. The sunlight bounced off the large crystal chandelier, casting an orange glow, making it feel more like a home than just a boat. Each piece of furniture looked like it was picked out by their own personal designer. I'd never seen anything like it. The floor-to-ceiling windows basked the entire interior with the warm light of the sun. The master bedroom was perfect, with its oversized sleigh bed facing the river. I could imagine myself watching a gorgeous sunset every single night through the beautiful bay windows.

Maverick's spirit seemed to improve as we walked through the enormous boat, each room just as impressive as the last. When we came to the last one, Maverick stopped at the doorway and stared at me while I looked at the large painting of sunflowers hanging on the wall.

"Thank you," I whispered as I walked over to him. "Not for the breaking and entering exactly, but the rest of it. Thanks for bringing me here. Showing me this place. It's really amazing."

"Come here," he demanded, his voice was low and filled with a hint of mischief. A thrill shot through me as I stepped closer to him, feeling the heat of his stare burn against my flesh. When I was face-to-face with him, I placed my palms flat against his chest, trying to steady myself from my shaky knees. His hands dropped to my waist, pulling me closer to him. He leaned over me, his lips trailing kisses down my neck.

He reached for the hem of my t-shirt, quickly pulling it over my head. As soon as my favorite, pink bra hit the floor, he kissed me – an aggressive, bruising, mind-blowing kiss. I wasn't patient. I needed to feel him against my body to ease the growing desire that was building in my stomach. My fingers slid up under his shirt, feeling the muscles of his stomach grow taut against the touch of my fingertips. I eased the soft fabric t-shirt over his head and tossed it towards the bed.

He was reaching for the button of my shorts when I said, "We're going to be in so much trouble if these people come home and find us here screwing around in their bed." It was a warning, but I didn't want to stop, stopping was the last thing I wanted to do. There was something about the thought of getting caught that actually enticed me even more.

"You'd like that, wouldn't you? Thinking about getting caught, turns you on, doesn't it?" he teased.

"Maybe," I confessed. The sound of his zipper sliding down sent a jolt of excitement through me. This man had me imagining all sorts of things – very naughty, wicked things. Unable to hide the thoughts that were going through my head, a devious smile crept across my face. I slowly dropped to my knees, reaching out for the waistband of his jeans. His eyes widened when I started to inch his jeans down his hips.

A torturous groan vibrated through his chest when I took him in my hand and began to stroke my hand up and down his hard, rigid shaft. His fingers clamped around the edge of the dresser, and his eyes shut when I brushed my tongue across the head of his dick.

"Fuck," he mumbled as I took him deep in my mouth. I continued to stroke him slowly, with my fingers wound tightly around his cock, feeling him throb against my tongue. His fingers tangled in my hair as his hips thrust forward, guiding me to take him deeper. I wasn't exactly confident that I was doing it right, but seeing how his body responded to my touch, gave me such a sense of power. The thought of making this man lose control with just my mouth exhilarated me, fueled my desire, and made me want him even more. With just the twist of my hand, a guttural moan echoed through the room and a pained expression crossed his face.

I loved seeing him fall apart by my touch, and I was shocked when I was suddenly yanked up from the floor and carried over to the bed. He dropped me, with my back lying flat against the mattress. I propped up on my elbows and watched him slowly lower my shorts down my legs.

"Hey!" I protested.

He whispered, "I love your mouth, Henley, but I want to be inside you when I cum."

I anxiously waited as he tore the condom wrapper with his teeth, and slowly slid the latex down his long, hard shaft. He hovered between my legs, and goosebumps rose from my flesh, while I watched his eyes roam over every inch of my bare skin.

"You're so fucking beautiful, Henley," he whispered, the heat of his breath caressing my neck.

His calloused thumb circled around my nipple, and my hips bucked towards him, needing to feel him inside me. "Please," I begged.

His warm, wet tongue pressed against my breast as he said, "Please what, Henley? Tell me what you want." He was teasing me with his words, driving me wild with anticipation.

"You, Logan. I want *you*," I purred. When I looked at him, his eyes were filled with hunger, hunger for me. It gave me a thrill to see him looking at me like that. My body shuddered beneath him, unable to withstand the intensity of his gaze. My heart pounded furiously in my chest, and, in that moment, I knew. Logan had stolen my heart, and there was nothing I could do about it. I loved him, body and soul. His eyes were still locked on mine, when he drove deep inside me… harder and faster than I expected. A strangled cry of relief got caught in my throat when he pulled out to the tip and then pushed back inside me. My nails dug into his back as I tilted my hips forward, welcoming his invasion. His eyes were locked on mine while he thrust inside of me, again and again. I slowly raised my knees up to his hips, pulling him deeper inside me. A low groan of pleasure vibrated through his chest as he steadied his stride, easing his rhythm to a slow, demanding pace.

I couldn't take it. I need more. All of his restraint began to vanish as my body started to tremble and writhe beneath him. With one hand on my hip and the other on my shoulder, he ground his hips against mine. A jolt of pleasure shot through me when he deepened the angle, making my body clamp down around him. The muscles in my body grew tight as my release began to build, burning deep in my stomach. I lifted my hips, trying to match his unrelenting rhythm, but it was too much. The warmth of his body, the consuming burn of his touch, sent me over the edge. My hands reached for the sheets at my side, fisting them tightly when my body began to tremble uncontrollably as my orgasm took hold.

"That's it, baby. I want to feel you cum. Your pussy is so fucking tight," he groaned, and just the sound of his voice sent me spiraling out of control. With a look of pure ecstasy on his face, he quickened his pace. I arched my back as my orgasm seized against my spine. He leaned over me, pressing his lips against mine, smothering my moans of ecstasy. Sweat trickled down his back while his body continued to pound into mine. I wound my legs around his hips, pulling him deeper inside me. With one last, powerful thrust, he found his own release. He held us there, motionless, until his body collapsed against mine.

Minutes passed and I was still trying to catch my breath. Finally, I whispered, "As much as I like having your hot, sweaty body on top of me, I… can't… breathe," I gasped. Smiling, he quickly rolled to the side and he pulled me over to him.

"Is that better?" he chuckled.

"Much," I laughed. The rumbles of voices outside the window stole my laughter and replaced it with panic. "Shit! They're here!"

Maverick jumped off the bed, revealing his perfectly round ass and long, muscular legs. He peered through the curtains, looking to see who was coming. "It's not them. It's just their neighbors, but we better get moving. It wouldn't be good for them to see us in here."

After putting on our clothes, we quickly made the bed, making sure not to leave any evidence of our little visit behind. When we finished, Maverick took my hand and led me down the hall. My nerves were on full alert, when he looked through the window one last time to make sure we were clear to leave. Thankfully, the neighbors were busy unloading groceries from their car and didn't see us slip out the back door.

When we stepped outside, it was almost noon, and the sun was barreling down on us as we walked down the dock. I wanted to jump into the lake and let the water cool my burning skin, but Maverick was still holding my hand, tugging me towards the car. I wasn't ready to go back to the clubhouse yet, so as soon as his car door slammed shut, I turned to him and asked, "How about something to eat? I'm starving."

"You're always starving. My girl and her snacks," he snickered. The sound of '*my girl*' rolling off of his lips made my heart flip inside of my chest. "We'll grab a burger at Hidden Creek on the way back to the club."

"Great," I told him smiling. I didn't care

where we went. I just wanted to keep him to myself, as long as I could.

After a few turns down a long, curvy road, we pulled up to a quaint little store with a small patio-styled bar attached on the side. There was a flashing sign out front announcing that there would be a band playing this weekend, and golf carts lined the front parking lot. When we opened the door, the smell of bacon whipped around me, making my stomach growl with hunger. We'd only been standing there for a few seconds when a young girl in her twenties came up and greeted us.

"I'll be with y'all in just a second. Make yourself comfortable," she said, forcing a smile as she motioned her hand towards the tables in the back corner of the room. Several older men were sitting around drinking coffee. Each one of them was leaned back in his chairs, reading the morning paper. I had no doubt that they came here every morning to start the day.

"They've got pretty good cheeseburgers, or bacon and eggs if you're still in the mood for breakfast," Maverick told me when we sat down at one of the empty tables.

"A cheeseburger sounds perfect. I want mine with the works," I told him. "I'm going to run to the bathroom. I'll be right back."

"It's down the hall on the right," Maverick told me, pointing down a long, dark hall. I was just about to open the bathroom door when I heard the waitress's voice coming through the wall. She was obviously upset, her voice getting higher and higher. No one was responding to her, so I assumed that she was talking on her cell phone.

"I told you months ago that I was done with your shit, Drew. Now, let it go! Stop calling me! Stop texting me. And for fuck's sake, stop coming by the house. If you haven't freaking noticed, I do **not** want to see you!" she barked. There was a brief pause before she started up again, "I don't give a shit! You're the one who decided to screw that whore from next door. That's all on you. I don't want to hear anything else you have to say. If you come around here again, I'm calling Bishop. Period." There was a little commotion coming from the restroom, and then, suddenly the door flew open.

Her face flushed red with embarrassment when she saw me standing there, and before I could tell her not to worry about it, she said, "Uh… sorry about that. I have the ex from hell, and he just doesn't know how to take no for an answer."

"No need to apologize. There's nothing worse than a guy like that, but it sounded like you handled him pretty well," I told her, smiling. She seemed like a really cool girl, and I hated that this guy was giving her such a hard time. She was a least a foot shorter than me, making her seem a little younger than she really was. Her hair was pulled back in a fishtail braid, and she was wearing a pair of shorts with a hot tank top that said, '*I'm actually not funny. I'm just mean and people think I'm joking*'. I wanted one, and if she hadn't been in the middle of an angry rant, I would have ask her where she'd gotten it.

"I'd really like to throat punch the asshole, but I doubt that it'd make much difference. We'd been dating for over a year when I found out he was screwing the slut-bag next door. I broke it off, but he just can't get it through his thick skull that I'm done with his dumbass," she explained as she let out a flustered sigh. "I'm sorry. I got carried away. It's just one of those days."

"No problem. We all have them," I said laughing.

"By the way, my name is Sunny."

"Nice to meet you, Sunny. I'm Henley. I'm here with Maverick," I told her as I looked back to our table. When I saw that Maverick was distracted with his phone, I asked her, "So, I heard you mention Bishop's name earlier. Do you know him?" I brought my hand up to my face, covering my eyes with my fingers while I shook my head. "I'm sorry. I shouldn't have asked… that's none of my business."

"Don't be silly. I basically just spilled my guts to you in the ladies restroom, so I'd say you're entitled to a question or two. I'm Bishop's neighbor. My mom used to babysit his son, Myles, so we're all pretty close. I'd never really call him over something like this, but I know he'd be there for me, if I really needed him," she explained.

"I'm sure he would. Be sure to let him know, if you keep having problems with this guy. Maybe he can do something to help you sort it."

"I will. I'd better get back up front before the lunch crowd starts rolling in," she told me as she started towards the front. She turned back to me and said, "It was really great meeting you. Next time you're in town, stop by, and I'll buy you a drink."

"That would be great, Sunny. I'll do that," I replied just before I walked into the restroom. By the time I came back, Maverick had already placed our order and our drinks were sitting on the table.

"Did you get lost?" he asked, putting his phone back in his pocket.

"I was just having a little chat with our waitress, Sunny. She's having some guy troubles," I told him.

"Did you get her sorted?" he asked with a mocking grin.

"From what I could tell, she did a pretty good job of sorting it herself," I explained. I looked back over to Sunny, hoping that I was right. She seemed like a really amazing girl, and I'd hate for anything to happen to her.

When we finished eating, Maverick stood up from the table and said, "We need to get back to the club. I texted Gavin to tell him that we were on our way. I'm not exactly looking forward to it, but it's time for us to talk."

I'd almost forgotten the hell that was waiting for Maverick when we got back to the club, but hearing Gavin's name tossed me right back into reality. Gavin had screwed up big time when he betrayed his brother, and I wondered if Maverick would ever be able to forgive him. I worried that after today, neither of them would ever be the same.

Chapter 19

MAVERICK

THE AIR WAS thick with tension when I walked into the empty bar. Gavin was sitting alone, lost in his thoughts while he took a drink from his beer. The stool screeched against the floor as I sat down next to him, and when he turned to face me, I could tell from the expression on his face that he was dreading this conversation almost as much as I was. We were both trying to face the demons from our past; things we wished we hadn't done, and it wasn't going to be easy for either of us. But then again, I wasn't the one who had been lying to my own flesh and blood for all these months, keeping secrets that no brother should've kept. Hell, I wanted him to dread it, to feel like the sorry bastard that he was. He's my fucking brother! He should have said something, and I doubted that I would ever be able to forgive him for keeping this from me. Things between us will never be the same, and he was going to have to live with that regret for the rest of his life.

"I'm sorry," he mumbled with his eyes full of remorse. "I don't know what else to say. I'm just so fucking sorry."

"How about you tell me how John Warren ended up being your son, Gavin? Why don't you tell me when you started fucking Hailey?" I growled. The anger inside of me was burning in my gut, and I wanted to beat the living hell out of him… tell him how he fucked it all up. I wanted to walk out of that bar and never speak to him again, but I needed to know the truth. I had to know what happened between him and Hailey.

"It was only that one night, Logan. I swear it. Hailey loved you. Loved you more than you ever really knew, but that night… she was just," he said, as he dropped his head into the palms of his hands.

"What night, Gavin?" I asked. When he didn't answer, I slammed my fist against the counter and shouted, "Tell me. What fucking night?"

He turned to look at me, and anguish rippled across his face as he said, "The night you caught her buying more drugs and walked out on her. I'm not saying it was the wrong thing for you to do, but it broke her. She was just so damn broken."

"So you fucked her? That was your answer to all her troubles? I was trying to make her see that she needed to get help, that she was going to kill herself if she kept that shit up, and you decide to go and fuck her. You thought that was going to make it all better?" I shouted. "That's just great, Gavin. You're the fucking hero." The sarcasm dripped from my mouth as I glared at him with all the rage that was building inside of me.

"It wasn't like that, Logan! You know I wouldn't … The guys and I had been watching the game, and I was already plastered when she got to the house. After they left, Hailey and I had a few drinks – more than a few. She was upset, and we spent the entire night talking about everything that had happened. There was so much pain in her voice. I hated to see her like that, and I wanted to help her."

He looked up to the ceiling, trying to reign in his emotions. Finally, he cleared his throat and continued, "She wanted to be the Hailey that you loved, but a part of her knew she'd never be that girl again. I'd never seen her so upset. She was just so heartbroken. You know I've always had a soft spot for Hailey, and I just wanted to help her, to be there for her." He took a long tug of his beer and let out a deep breath.

"Why didn't you just tell me? You knew the hell I was going through, and you never said a goddamn thing! That's bullshit, Gavin. I should've been able to trust you more than anyone, but you lied to me to protect your own sorry ass. There's no excuse. You should've said something!" I told him.

"Maverick, I don't even remember what happened that night. It was all just a blur. The more we talked, the angrier she got. The angrier she got, the more she drank. We were both completely wasted, and when I woke up the next morning, she was gone. I couldn't remember a damn thing. I wasn't even sure that we had actually slept together. I prayed that we didn't. I hated myself for putting myself in that situation, but you have to know that I would never intentionally hurt you or her." He looked up to me, glaring at me with hurt in his eyes and said, "I should've told you, Maverick. I'm sorry. I really am. It was only one night, and I really thought he was your kid."

My anger slowly started to subside as I listened to him talk, knowing that he really was struggling with his guilt. I could see the grief written all over his face, and I knew he would never intentionally set out to hurt either of us. Gavin was just a kid, and Hailey should've never gone over there that night.

I rested my hand on his shoulder and said, "I knew she was upset the night I left. I've always hated myself for not staying with her and making sure that she got the help she needed," I told him.

"No. It wasn't your fault, none of it. Hailey's the one who got behind the wheel that night. She was tired, and never saw that drunk driver heading in her direction. It was an accident. You can't keep blaming yourself for that night."

"Maybe."

"And her addiction was just that – hers. She knew that you loved her and that should've been enough. That's all on her, Maverick." I knew there was some truth in the words that he was saying, but I wasn't willing to let myself truly accept it. A part of me would always blame myself for what happened with Hailey. No one would change my mind about that.

"I'm just so tired. Tired of it all, and I'm done with it. Done with the lies, the guilt. No more, Gavin," I told him, dragging my hands through my hair. I was so fucking tired of being angry. Tired of all the bullshit. It was wearing me down, and I had to let it go. At the end of the day, Gavin was my brother. I knew I'd never be able to forget what he did, but I had to forgive him. I had to forgive myself.

His hand rested on my back as he assured me, "No more."

"I mean it, Gavin. You fucked up. We're family, we don't keep shit from each other. Period."

"You're right. You have my word. I'll never

make a mistake like that again," Gavin promised.

I was just about to leave when I realized that I still didn't know what transpired after I left the lawyer's office. "What happened today with John Warren?"

"I went down to the hospital, and Ana did another DNA test. When the results come back, I'll sign the adoption papers," Gavin replied. "Even if I was in a position to be a father, I wouldn't do anything different. We both know that JW is where he belongs."

"It'll be hard, but, at least, you'll be here with him. You'll get the chance to see him grow up and spend time with him. You can be a real part of his life, and he'll be lucky to have you," I told him.

"Maverick, you should know that I had no idea that I was John Warren's father when I decided to come here. I honestly thought being here would help you, make it easier for you somehow."

"At the time, it did make me feel better to know that you'd be here with him. I think this place has been good for both of you," I told him. I got up to grab a beer from the cooler, but stopped when my phone started to ring. I pulled it from my pocket and saw that it was Big Mike.

I didn't have a chance to say hello before he said, "We've got a problem, Maverick. How soon can you get back?"

"Hold on," I told him as I walked outside for some privacy. The door slammed behind me when I stepped out onto the gravel parking lot and asked, "What's going on?"

"It's Nitro… They got to Nitro," he said, his voice rattled with concern.

"What do you mean they got to Nitro?" I asked, pacing back and forth.

"We still don't know all of the details. Just that he was shot four to five times at one of his warehouses. The doctors just got done working on him a few minutes ago. He's in the ICU now. They're not sure if he'll make it."

"Nitro is too fucking stubborn to die, brother. He'll pull through. Any idea who did it?"

"You know who fucking did it, Maverick. The same fuckers that were taking those pictures at our last delivery. They were looking for our distributor. They're not going to stop until they shut us down," he explained.

"That's not going to happen. I won't let it."

"We've got to find these fuckers. We just need to get our hands on one of them. Just one of them, and Stitch will do the rest. He'll get what we need out of them," he explained.

"Yeah, one would do it." Just thinking about the methods Stitch used to get information sent cold chills down my spine. One night in the confines of that room, and he could break any man. Mike was right. All we had to do was get our hands on one of these guys, and Stitch would find out everything we needed to know.

"We've talked about it before. They aren't the type to leave any loose ends, and letting Henley slip through their fingers had to piss them off. There's no reason for us not to use that to our advantage."

"I've already told you once that using Henley is not an option, Mike. I won't say it again," I shouted. I took a deep breath and said, "We'll be on the road within the hour. We'll discuss other options when I get back."

"Yeah. I'll see you then," he mumbled. I could hear the frustration in his voice, but I knew one way or another, we'd find a way to get these guys. When I turned to go back inside, Henley was standing behind me with her hands shoved deep in her pockets.

"Is everything okay?" she asked as she shifted her feet across the gravel. I wasn't exactly sure, but I had a feeling she'd heard the entire conversation.

"We've got to head back."

"You didn't answer my question," Henley grumbled, moving her hands up to her hips. I loved that she didn't back down from me. She knew what she wanted, and she didn't have a problem going after it. Unfortunately for her, I wasn't telling her a damn thing.

"Go pack," I told her. She looked up at me

through her long, dark eyelashes, pouting because she knew she wasn't going to get her way. I leaned down and quickly pressed my lips against hers. Her pout began to fade when I said, "We really need to get going."

"Okay," she replied with a defeated sigh. She followed me back to the room, and after packing our bags, we headed to the bar to tell everyone goodbye.

Gavin was the only one still around, so I told him, "We're heading home. I'll try to get back soon." I wanted to be able to stay for a little longer to be there for him, while he got this mess sorted with John Warren, but I didn't have a choice. I had to get back.

"Maybe I can make it back for a couple of days before Thanksgiving. The holidays are busy, so I won't be able to stay long," Gavin explained.

"Come whenever you can. It'd be good to see you," I told him as I gave him a hug. "Let me know how things go with Lily and Goliath."

"I will. Be careful driving back," he said smiling. "And Henley… try to make him stop from time to time. He'll drive all the way through if you let him."

"I'll try, but you know he has a stubborn streak a mile long," she laughed. She hugged him quickly before we headed to the car.

For the first two hours of the drive back, Henley never stopped talking. She asked a million questions about Bishop and the Devil Chasers, and wouldn't stop prodding until I told her everything I could about them. She was disappointed that she didn't have a chance to meet them all, but I assured her that we would be back. When she had her fill of the club, she started talking about Courtney. She couldn't stop laughing when she told me all the funny things she'd said when they were out shopping. It was obvious that she'd had a good time with them, and I looked forward to bringing her back.

Eventually, the day caught up with her; she yawned and stretched before resting her head on my thigh. I gently ran my fingers through her long brown hair while she drifted off to sleep. I took a deep breath, inhaling her soft scent, and it helped calm the storm of thoughts that were rushing through my head. Even with all the shit that was going down with the club, having her next to me gave me a sense of peace that I couldn't explain. I didn't know when it happened... or *how* it happened, but this woman had stolen my heart. I knew I couldn't fight it any longer, and honestly, I didn't want to. She was mine, and I wouldn't have it any other way.

Chapter 20

HENLEY

THE CAR WAS quiet as I laid there with my head resting in Maverick's lap. I was so tired, but I just couldn't make myself fall asleep. My eyes were closed, and I could feel him playing with a strand of my hair while he drove. I desperately wanted to sleep – needed to sleep, but I couldn't stop thinking about that phone conversation I'd overheard with Maverick and Big Mike. I knew there was something going on with the club, and it was bad. It was something that threatened to tear them apart, but Maverick refused to tell me what was going on. I knew that there would always be secrets with the club… things Maverick just couldn't tell me, but I wasn't expecting to hear him growl out my name like that to Big Mike. He was pissed when he told Mike that I wasn't an option. He demanded that they find another way. A way to do what? I had no idea what he was talking about, but I knew I had to find out.

When I finally woke up, the sun was just be-ginning to rise over the horizon. I looked over to Maverick, and his eyes were red with exhaustion, and his eyelids were heavy and dark. "You need to get some sleep," I told him.

"We'll stop in an hour for breakfast. I'll get some coffee when we get there," he grumbled.

"Pull over," I demanded. "Let me drive for a while."

I expected him to fight me… to tell me to piss off, but he slowly pulled the car over onto the shoulder of the highway, letting me take the wheel. I reached in the backseat and grabbed my jacket, folding it neatly into a pillow for him. I put it on my lap and waited for him to lay down. The minute his head hit my make-shift pillow, he was sound asleep. I even managed to slip through a drive-through without waking him up.

The entire time I was driving, I was thinking about Maverick. He'd been through so much over the past year, and things were finally coming together for him. If he could get this mess settled with his club, he could have a real chance to be free, to really be happy. I wanted to do some-thing to help him, to help the club catch the guys that were giving them so much hell. I needed to talk to Big Mike. He wouldn't have brought my name up, if there wasn't something I could do to help. I knew Maverick wouldn't want me to get involved, but I needed to do this.

It was almost noon when the gas tank ran low, forcing me to stop. When I turned off the engine, Maverick ran his hands over his face as he sat up in his seat. He sat there staring out the window in a daze, and I hated that I had to wake him up.

"Hey there, sleepyhead," I said softly.

He groaned while he stretched out his arms and said, "What time is it?"

"It's almost twelve. We've made good time, and should be home in about eight hours."

"Thanks for driving. I'll get the gas. You go grab us something to eat, real food. Not that junk food shit you live on," he said sarcastically.

"I'll see what they've got," I said, smirking as I got out of the car. Luckily there was a burger place attached to the convenience store, so I was able to get us both a decent lunch. I also grabbed a few snack essentials just in case we didn't make another stop.

When I came back outside, Maverick was already sitting in the driver's seat and ended up driving the rest of the way home. He drove with a heavy foot, so we made it in seven hours instead of eight. As soon as we'd unpacked the car, Maverick told me that he needed to go have a word with Cotton. The minute he left, I set out to find Big Mike. I worried that this might be my only opportunity to talk to him without Maverick knowing.

When he opened his door, he looked surprised to see me standing there. He cleared his throat and said, "I didn't know that you had made it back. Where's Maverick?"

"He went to talk to Cotton. If you've got a minute, I'd like to ask you about something."

"Okay? Come on in," he said as he stepped out of the doorway.

"So… Maverick told me about your idea?" I lied. I knew he wouldn't talk to me about it, otherwise. His eyebrows pinched together as he struggled with whether he should believe me or not. He was struggling and didn't know what to say.

"Well, he didn't like the idea, so there's no point talking about it," he said, turning away from me.

"Come on, Mike. Don't be like that. I really think this could solve everything. We'd just need to figure out how this whole thing would work," I explained. I still had no idea what I was talking about, but I could see the wheels start to turn behind his eyes.

"Maverick will shit a brick if he finds out I'm even talking to you about this," he grumbled.

"Yeah, well, what else is new? He has a conniption fit about everything," I said smiling. I didn't like keeping this from Maverick, but I didn't know any other way. "I just don't see how it could work?"

"It's a stupid idea, Henley. It's just too dangerous. Maverick was right, using you just isn't an option."

"I think you both are wrong about that," I snapped.

"It is too dangerous. Using you as bait was a stupid idea, and who knows if that tracker on your car is still working? And even if we were there waiting for them, it is just too risky. Anything could happen."

"That's the one thing that I don't understand. Why would they still want me? I don't really have anything to do with your club."

"These men are different, Henley. Whoever they are, they aren't the kind of people who like to leave loose ends. You're the only one who can tie them to Skidrow's murder, and they won't want to take a chance on you burning them later down the road."

It made sense, but I still found it hard to believe that these men would really come after me. "What does Cotton think about your idea?"

"I haven't said anything to him. Maverick…"

"I'm not telling you to go against Maverick. I know you aren't in the position to do that. It would take a lot to change his mind, but if you think it's a good idea, you should push for it. I am willing to do whatever the club needs me to do."

"Henley, just let it go. I've already told you. These men are dangerous. They aren't the kind of guys you mess around with or you could end up getting yourself killed. Maverick's right. We'll find another way," he warned.

"Okay, maybe you are right." I could hear it in his voice that he had no intention of going against Maverick. I didn't blame him. No one wanted to piss him off, especially me.

It was well after midnight when Maverick finally came to bed. The sounds of his snoring echoed through the room, but I didn't have the heart to nudge him. He'd had such a long day, and the deep sleep would do him good. The air conditioner was set on high, so the room was absolutely freezing. My toes felt like ice as I snuggled up beside him, enjoying the heat that radiated off of his warm body. Once I was able to stop my jaw from chattering, I closed my eyes and tried to welcome the exhaustion that was overtaking my body. I just wanted to sleep, to forget all the thoughts that were racing through my head. Unfortunately, I couldn't stop thinking about what Big Mike had said. There had to be a way to make his plan work without really putting myself in danger. When I couldn't think of a safe plan, one that didn't involve me getting brutally murdered, I gave up and finally went to sleep.

Sometime in the middle of the night, I felt Maverick kissing along my neck. He continued to nip and suck along my neck and shoulder, while he eased my lace panties down my hips. My back was pressed against his chest as I pushed my ass back against his hard cock. That's all it took. We spent the next hour making love, and the world around us disappeared. There were no thoughts of Tennessee or overheard phone conversations. It was just him and me, and nothing else mattered. I loved him. He made me feel safe and secure, and being wrapped up in his arms was the only place I wanted to be.

I was still in a sex-induced coma when Maverick gave me a swift slap against my ass and said, "Hey, Slick. I'll be back in a couple of hours."

He'd just gotten out of the shower, and his tousled wet hair fell low across his eyebrows. His black t-shirt hugged across his chest, showing off his broad shoulders, and his faded jeans fell just below his hips. Just seeing him standing there looking so damn gorgeous snapped me out of my haze. "Wait! Where are you going?" I tried to rub the sleep out of my eyes as I sat up in the bed.

"Heading over to the hospital. I've got someone I need to see."

I didn't miss the lack of information he'd just provided, like who he was going to see and why, so I hesitated for just a minute before I asked, "Mind if I tag along?"

"You going to behave?" he smirked.

"Maverick, I *always* behave. Now, can I go or not?" I said, giving him my most innocent smile.

"You can come, but you'll have to hang back while I go inside," he told me, crossing his arms across his chest. "It's business, Henley. No fucking around."

"Yes, Boss. I'll do anything you tell me to."

"Hmmm… anything?" he growled. "I'll take you up on that when we get back." His lips crashed against mine as he pulled me to my feet, kissing me with such passion and heat that my knees buckled beneath me. He held me close to his chest, claiming me with his mouth. I was about to melt there on the spot, when he pulled himself from our embrace. "We need to go," he said, smacking me on the ass again.

"You're going to pay for that mister!" I told him with my finger pointed towards him. I shook my head as I walked to the bathroom to get ready to go. "Totally going to pay."

"Bring it on, Slick," he taunted before I closed the door behind me.

Once I was dressed, I followed him out to his bike. He held out his hand to me, helping me get on behind him. I fastened my helmet while he started up the engine, and within seconds, we were out on the main road. I loved riding with him. There was nothing like being so close to him as he sped through the traffic. I'd never felt so alive, and I was almost disappointed when he pulled into the hospital parking lot.

Just as we were stepping off the elevator, Maverick turned to me and said, "His room is down the hall. You can just hang out in the waiting room."

"Okay."

"I won't be long," he assured me.

He kissed me quickly on the lips before he headed down the hall. When he disappeared into the hospital room, I went to the waiting room and sat down in the only empty seat. After flipping through the pages of three different magazines, I began to get restless. I tried to be patient... tried to do what he told me to, but I couldn't stop wondering who was lying in that hospital bed. When I couldn't take it any longer, I got up from my seat, and slowly walked out of the crowded waiting room. The hallway seemed so much longer than it did thirty minutes ago, and I was having a hard time remembering where he turned to go into that room. I was about to give up and go back to the waiting room when I heard Maverick. His voice was low, but I could tell that he was upset.

When I stepped up to the glass window, and peered into the room, I saw Maverick try to console his hurting friend. I'd never seen this man before, so I knew he wasn't one of Maverick's brothers. I had no idea what had happened to him, but it was obviously bad – very bad. His face was deathly pale, and he was covered in bandages. He looked like he was in horrible pain as he laid there listening to Maverick. Every so often, he would wince when he struggled to respond to Maverick. He could barely talk, barely move as Maverick tried to talk to him. My chest tightened when I realized that he didn't have cuts or scratches. There were no signs of bruising that might have come from some sort of accident. He'd been shot – more times than I could count. When I looked over to Maverick and saw the look of anguish on his face, I wanted to go to him, try to comfort him, but I knew I couldn't. I had to get back to the waiting room before he saw me.

I rushed back to my seat in the waiting room, and tried shake the image of what I had seen from my mind. I couldn't stop obsessing over the bullet wounds that covered the man's body. Who could have done that to him? Was it the same men that killed Skidrow? I wasn't sure how, but the man lying in that hospital bed had to have some tie to the club, and it scared me. Things weren't getting any better, and I wished there was something I could do to help them.

Chapter 21

MAVERICK

N ITRO WASN'T MUCH help. He was still in a lot of pain, and it was hard for him to talk about it. He told me it was dark, and he couldn't see who it was that shot him. It was bugging the shit out of him that he didn't know more. In all the years Satan's Fury has been working with him, this was the first time anyone had gotten past his long line of artillery. Nitro was the kind of man who always covered his tracks, never letting anyone fuck with him, and he was pissed that someone managed to catch him off guard. Considering how much protection he had, I could only assume that Nitro was shot by someone using a long distance rifle. It was the only way they'd ever be able to get a decent shot. Seeing him laid up in that hospital bed, actually made me feel a little sorry for the guy. He'd always been a pain in the ass, but he was good at his job. After all this, I knew he'd tighten up the reigns, making it even harder to deal with him.

Over the past few days, the club had met time and time again trying to find some kind of strategy. This shit was getting serious, and we had no idea what these guys were going to do next. Cotton was on edge, and the tension among the brothers was growing out of control. I needed a fucking break, so I headed into the kitchen for something to eat. When I walked into the kitchen, I found Dusty sitting at the table alone.

"Hey, little brother. What's up?" I asked, with a chin lift as I pulled up a chair and sat down next to him. His eyebrows pinched together, making him look agitated.

"Nutin'," he mumbled.

I was surprised to see him sitting there alone, so I asked, "Where's your mom?"

"She's talkin' to Cotton," he told me as he took a bite of his peanut butter and jelly sandwich. Something was wrong. He didn't plow into me with a hug. Hell, he wouldn't even look at me, and that just wasn't like him.

"You want to tell me what's bugging you?" I asked.

"No…" he pouted.

"Come on, Dusty. You know you can talk to me about it. Tell me what's wrong."

He let out a little defeated sigh before he said, "It was a girl in my class. She was really mean to me today," he told me with his eyes skirting down towards his lap.

"Oh yeah… how was she mean?"

"She told me that I looked stupid… that I was stupid," he cried. "She hit me in my arm really hard and called me retarded."

"I'm sorry about that, Dusty. You're right… that was mean. She doesn't seem like a very nice girl to be saying something like that to you," I told him. I hated that he had to deal with such ignorant people, but I knew it would only get worse as he got older. Dusty was an amazing kid, and if people would just give him a chance, they'd just see a special kid.

"Mom said that girl had a small mind like her momma," he said. His eyes darted up to mine, searching for some kind of affirmation that his mother was right.

"Your mom's right. That little girl is small minded, so I guess that makes her the one who's not very smart," I said trying my best to smile. "Fourth grade is tough. You just need to forget about what that little girl said and just be yourself. If she doesn't want to be your friend, then it's her loss."

"Okay. Did you get any sprinkles?" he asked with his eyes sparkling with excitement. And just like that, he was moving on.

"I did. Finish your lunch, and I'll make you some ice cream."

Dusty was almost finished eating his ice cream when Dallas walked in. Her mascara was running down her cheeks, and she was carrying a balled up tissue in her hand. She stopped before Dusty caught sight of her, and tried to clear the traces of her tears, but it was no use. She was a mess.

"Dallas? What's wrong?" I asked as I stood up and walked over to her.

"I'm fine… it's nothing," she said as she wiped her nose.

"Dallas…" I started.

"It's that damn insurance company. They're still giving me a hard time, and it's just wearing me out. We're not hurting for money, at least not yet, but Dusty's behavioral therapist is expensive. His bills add up fast. Daniel wanted the kids to have that insurance money for their future, and those assholes are trying to keep it from them," she snapped.

"Anything I can do?"

"Thanks, but Cotton is looking into it. He said he might be able to contact some resources."

"Good. Be sure to let me know if you need anything. All you have to do is ask," I told her.

"I know that, Maverick. I really appreciate you being so good to Dusty. He's had a hard day today, and he loves being with you."

"I like hanging out with him, too," I said smiling. "Don't worry about the money, Dallas.

We'll work it out."

"Thanks, Maverick. I better get going. Katie has a game tonight, and she'll freak if I'm late," she said as she reached up and gave me a quick hug. "Come on, buddy. We've got to hurry." She took him by the hand and led him out of the kitchen.

I was opening up the refrigerator when I felt Dusty's body slam across my back. His little arms wrapped tightly around my waist as he said, "Bye, Mav-wreck." He quickly let go and ran out the door. Damn, I loved that kid. He was just the distraction that I needed. For the first time since we'd got home, I had something to smile about.

After I finished my lunch, I went to my room looking for Henley. She was lying in the bed reading one of her books, and I was tempted to lay down with her. Unfortunately, I didn't have the time.

"I've got some club business to see about, so I'll be gone for a few hours," I told her.

"Okay," she said, never looking up from her book.

"It shouldn't take long."

"Okay," she mumbled as her eyes remained focused on her book.

"I might get attacked and eaten alive by a pack of wild beavers."

"Okay," she whispered as her teeth grazed across her bottom lip. Yeah. She was fucking with me.

"Alright, check ya later," I told her as I took a step towards the door. When she still didn't look over to me, I lunged towards her, pouncing right on top of her, and pinned her hands to the bed. Her eyes widened with surprise as her book went sailing across the room. "Are you pouting, Henley Gray?"

"Maybe," she whispered as she gave me her best puppy dog eyes.

I leaned down and pressed my lips to hers before I said, "You missing me, Henley?"

She rolled her eyes and said, "Ummm… nooo. I'm not."

"Yeah, you're missing me," I teased as I ground my hips against hers. When she bucked against me, I asked, "You miss my mouth, don't you, baby?"

"Ummm… maybe a little," she admitted as she squirmed beneath me.

"You want to feel my cock deep inside you, don't you?" I asked, rocking against her.

A deep, frustrated sigh vibrated through her chest as she said, "Yes!"

"Good," I taunted her as I pulled myself up off the bed. "I like you missing me. Now, behave until I get back."

"Maverick?" she called out. "I've been think-ing…" her voice trailed off as she thought about what she was about to say. "I know you've been having a hard time finding the guys that shot Skidrow, and I imagine they had something to do with your friend being in the hospital. I'd like to do something to help."

"Henley, I should tan that pretty little ass of yours for even thinking about this. Trust me. I'll take care of it," I assured her. "Gotta go. Let Smokey or Boozer know if you need anything. The rest of the guys will be out."

"Okay. Please be careful," she pleaded.

"Always," I assured her as I walked out of the room. I'd meant it when I told her that I liked her missing me. I hadn't had much time to spend with her over the past couple of days, and I liked the thought of her thinking about me, longing for me to hold her, to love on her. Amidst all the turmoil that'd thrown her into my life, she'd given me a light that I'd never known possible. I was missing her, too, and I was looking forward to making up for lost time as soon as I got back tonight.

Chapter 22

HENLEY

I HATED WATCHING Maverick walk out that door. I wanted to call him back, beg him to stay there with me, but I knew it was no use. He had so much going on with the club that I'd barely seen him over the past couple of days. I had too much time on my hands, and I was going insane. I felt useless. Having been around the brothers since the shooting, I'd come to really care for them. I was so tired of seeing the guys stressed. Their tension was palpable. Mostly, I missed Maverick. I craved the feeling of knowing he was always near me. I'd never had or wanted such undivided attention from a man.

I couldn't stop thinking about that guy in the hospital. Everything was going to shit, and I couldn't take it anymore. I had been thinking about this for days, and it was time to take a chance. I needed to do this for Maverick.

I had no idea what time he would be back, so

I didn't waste any time. If my plan was going to work, I would need Cassidy's help, so I went to see if she was at the bar. Thankfully, she was there filling the beer cooler when I walked up. "Hey, Sis! You got a minute?"

"What's up?"

"I really need to talk to you about something," I told her after a quick glance around the room, ensuring we wouldn't be overheard. "You're not going to like it, Cass, but I really need your help with something."

She came around the bar and sat down on a stool beside me. As I started to explain my plan, Cassidy's body grew tense with worry. When I was almost done talking, she sat up straight in her chair and leaned forward. She glared at me with an expression of total disbelief, as she tried to make sense of what I was saying.

Her face flushed red as she spat, "Have you lost your damn mind? Do you honestly think that I would help you get yourself killed? What kind of sister do you think I am? Hell will freeze over before I help you do this!"

"Cassidy… I love him… I really love him. Do you honestly think I want to go get myself killed now that I finally found the one? If we play this thing right, we can help them get these guys. But, I can't do it without you. I need your help with this. It's the only way. I've thought it through. You have to trust me."

"I just don't know, Henley. What if something goes wrong? I'll never be able to forgive myself if something happens to you," she said. However, I could tell by the sound of her voice that she was about to give in.

"We'll get in and we'll get out. Just trust me on this."

"Fine… I'll help you, but I'm not happy about it." Filled with relief that she agreed to help me, I jumped up and hugged her tightly.

"Thanks, Sis. I knew I could count on you," I whispered. "We need to go before Maverick gets back. Let me go get my stuff, and I'll meet you in your room in five minutes."

After I grabbed my purse, I headed down the hall to Cassidy's room. I didn't take time to think about what we were about to do. I knew I just had to swallow my nerves and get this thing done. I walked into her room. She was sitting on the edge of her bed, waiting with a pained expression on her face.

"Don't go backing out on me now, Cass. This is a good plan."

"I'm not backing out, Lee Bug. I'm just worried, that's all. Come on," she said as she stood up and reached for her keys. "Let's get this thing over with."

Cassidy was quiet while she drove me to the campus parking lot. My car was still parked in the front row of the Fine Arts Building. It had been sitting there since the day Clutch took me to the club. I prayed that the tracking device was still there and working. It was the only way they'd know that I had returned home.

I put my things in my car and sat down in the driver's seat. I looked up at Cassidy and said, "I'll park the car in my usual spot. You pull around back and wait for me there. I'll come down the fire escape once I get everything ready."

"What if someone is already there waiting for you? This is crazy, Henley. I should've never agreed to go along with this."

"No one is going to be there, at least not yet. Now, stop worrying."

"That's easier said than done. Just make it fast, okay?" she said with a shaky voice.

"Promise. I'll call you once I am inside, so we can talk the entire time I'm in there," I assured her.

My mind was racing as I drove to my apartment. I tried building up my courage by reminding myself that I was doing this for Maverick, for the man that I loved. Unfortunately, it didn't help settle the nerves that were causing my hands to tremble against the steering wheel. I took a deep breath, and tried to concentrate on all the things I needed to do. I tried to convince myself that there wasn't much to it. I just had to park the car in front of the apartment and then, rush inside to get everything ready. I needed to try to make the place look like I was returning home. I needed to turn on the lights and TV, straighten the place up a bit, and then arrange the bed to look like I was lying under the covers. Once everything was set up, I'd slip out the back down the fire escape. Cass would be waiting for me in her car, and we'd wait to see if anyone showed up. The plan was simple. The problem was nothing with me ever seemed to go like it was supposed to.

Several cars were parked in front of my small apartment complex, but thankfully my spot was still empty. I eased the car into park and slowly opened my door, looking around for anything that might seem suspicious. The streetlights gave off just enough light to create an eerie feel to the entire parking lot. I really wasn't sure what I should be looking for, but I let my eyes roam over the area, hunting for anything or anyone that might be lurking in the dark. I was still searching the area, for God knows what, while I walked up the steps that led up to the front door.

Before I walked inside, I looked back to make sure Cassidy was pulling her car around back. After I saw her taillights heading down the back alley, I stepped anxiously through the door. My legs felt heavy as I walked over to the main elevator. I tried to push back my terror as the doors closed behind me. There was no time to let my fears get in the way. I had no idea if that tracking device on my car was actually even working, but I didn't want to take any chances. If these guys think I'm back home, who knows how long it will take for them to come looking for me.

When the elevator doors opened, I stepped out into the empty hallway and crept over to my door. I didn't know what to expect, but I never thought it would be like this. I felt like an intruder in my own home as I unlocked my door. The familiar smell of lavender and fabric softener surrounded me as the door creaked open, but being there didn't feel familiar. I was scared. I felt so out of place, and I hated that I felt such fear in a place that I'd always loved to be.

As promised, I took out my phone, and called Cassidy. "I'm here."

"Please hurry, Henley," she pleaded.

"I've got to straighten up a bit. Just hold tight," I told her as I looked around the room. Several of my school papers were scattered along the floor, along with several overturned lamps and chairs. I quickly started cleaning up the mess, trying to make it resemble the place I'd called home for the past three years.

Once I had everything picked up, I turned on several more lights and the TV, setting the volume loud enough for it to be heard out in the hallway. My adrenaline was in overdrive as I raced to my room, and stuffed several pillows under the comforter. I tried my best to make it look like a body was lying there under the covers. I happened to remember a wig Cassidy bought the year we decided to be twins for Halloween, so I pulled the old costume box out from under the bed, hoping the wig was still there. Luckily, I found it buried at the bottom of the box. I quickly grabbed it and kicked the box back under the bed. I placed the wig at the top of the pillows, spreading out the hair in hopes it'd help, but I wasn't sure anyone would truly believe it was me. I glanced around my small apartment. Everything was set.

I picked back up my phone and said, "Cass… you there?"

"Yes! Are you done?" she asked.

"Yeah, I'm on my way down."

"Keep your phone on until you get in the car," she ordered. "And be careful."

"Okay. I'm coming now," I told her as I eased the window up leading to the fire escape. Holding tightly to the ledge, I stepped out onto the railing.

The stairs clattered and shook as I ran down the steps, and I thought I had made it free and clear, until I saw a man standing in the shadows. I froze. Panic surged through my body when I realized that he was staring right at me. My breathing became rapid, and I thought I might pass out from fear, but I took a deep breath, forcing myself to stay calm. There was still a chance that I could make it to the car without him catching me, so I took another step down the stairs. When I did, he began walking towards me... "Holy shit! Cass! Someone's here!" I whispered into my phone.

"Get your ass to the car! Now!" she cried.

"I can't! He's coming this way! Call Maverick. Call him, *now*!" I was in trouble. He was one of them. I'd run out of time, and there was no one here to help me.

Chapter 23

MAVERICK

Henley was nowhere to be found, and I was getting pissed. I told Smokey to keep an eye on her, but he had no idea where she'd run off to. I would have to deal with him later. I figured she must be somewhere with Cassidy, so I headed to Big Mike's room. He'd be able to trace her in a matter of seconds. I had lifted my hand to knock on the door when my cell phone rang.

Before I could answer, Cassidy started screaming, "You've got to get over here! Now! He's going to get her! He's so close. Oh my god, Maverick!"

"Slow down! Tell me what's going on!" I demanded. Hearing the panic in her voice made my heart pound against my chest.

"There's no time! He's about to get Henley. She's trying to get down the fire escape, and he's about to get her!" she cried hysterically. The

sound of Henley's name made my heart stop
beating in my chest. I needed a minute to think,
to focus on what she was saying.

"What fire escape?"

"The one at our apartment. She was trying to
help you, and…"

"I'm on my way," I snapped. Without knocking, I opened Big Mike's door and shouted, "Get
your ass up. Now!"

He turned from his computer and asked,
"What the hell, man?"

"Gather up the guys! Henley is in trouble.
We've got to get over to her place! NOW!" I
shouted. I couldn't hear his response over the
loud beating of my heart, as I went along the hall,
pounding on all the doors until I got to Cotton's
room. I knocked as I opened the door, not even
giving him a chance to acknowledge my presence
and said, "We got trouble."

"And?" he questioned as he stood up to face
me.

"Henley… Cass just called. They are at their
apartment, and they've got company. We've got
to get over there," I told him as my voice rattled
with nerves. None of this made any fucking
sense! Why? Why would she do this? Just a few
hours ago she was lying in the bed kissing me,
and now I might lose her. I might fucking lose
her!

"Don't… don't go thinking the worst…

We'll get her," he assured me.

"I won't lose her," I told him as I headed for my bike. This was my fault. I should've talked to her, explained how things worked in the club. I was too fucking stubborn, and now it might be too late.

With my brothers following close behind, I raced over to Henley's apartment. The road blurred before me as my imagination ran wild thinking about what might be happening to her. I pushed the throttle forward, increasing my speed to a dangerous level, but I didn't give a fuck. I had to get to her. It was the only thing that mattered.

The loud rumble of our engines had to draw the attention of everyone in that apartment complex, but there was no time to go in quiet. Every second counted, and we were running out of time. When we parked our bikes in front of her apartment, there was no one in sight. I instantly spotted Henley's car, but there was no sign of Cassidy anywhere. I turned back to Clutch and said, "Cassidy... find her."

"Cooter and I will check around back," he told me as they walked towards the back alley leading to the back of the building.

"Let's move it," I ordered, and my brothers followed me into the apartment building. While Cotton and I took the elevator, Guardrail led the others up the stairwell. I only had one thought on my mind as I waited for the doors to open… get to Henley. I prayed that I wasn't too late.

Chapter 24

HENLEY

I WAS SO close… just a few steps away from the car when his hand reached out and grabbed me. I tried to jerk free, pulling as hard as I could, but it was no use. I expected him to kill me right there, end this thing once and for all. But seconds later, my feet were dragging against the pavement. He reeked of sweat and cigarettes as he pulled me closer to him. My shoes clanked loudly against the metal steps as he yanked me towards the top of the fire escape. I didn't make it easy for him. I kicked. I screamed. I tried to claw myself from his arms, but it was no use… I couldn't get away. When he finally managed to get me back inside my apartment, I panicked. I knew my time was running out.

My back was pressed firmly against his chest with his arms wrapped tightly around my waist. I couldn't breathe. He was so much stronger than I was, and there was little I could do to keep him from squeezing the life out of me. I kept trying to fight him, doing anything I could to work myself free. I could feel my blood pulsing in my temples. My eyes were blurred with tears as he tightened his grip around my chest. I tried to call out for help, but nothing came. I couldn't get enough air into my lungs to even make a sound… not a cry… not even a whimper. I knew I had to do something. I had to try to get away from him before it was too late, so using everything I had, I reared my elbow back, slamming it into his lower abdomen. The heat of his breath blew against my neck and with a loud grunt, he loosened his hold. I was finally able to get away from him. Tears streamed down my face as I gasped and coughed, trying to fill my lungs with air.

"She's a feisty, little thing, isn't she?" a man snickered from behind me. I didn't have to turn around to know who the man was. I would never forget the sound of that voice. Still panting for breath, I turned to face him. His arms were crossed over his chest, and I instantly recognized the python tattoo that wrapped around his arm. It was him. The man that killed Skidrow.

"You bitch," the man next to me growled as he straightened his stance. "You little, fucking bitch. You're going to pay for that shit." He glared at me with such anger, such hate that it made my blood run cold. He wanted me dead.

Plain and simple.

He stalked towards me with his hand raised into a fist, and I saw it coming, but I was too dazed to react. The blow to the side of my face was so powerful, that I momentarily lost my vision. I was reaching out for something to grab onto, when he came at me again. I knew it was coming… I could hear the sounds of his feet shuffling towards me, but there was nothing I could do about it. I felt suspended in time, everything became a blur. He hit me with such force that my head jerked back, and I lost my footing. With my arms flailing in the air, I fell back and my head collided against the kitchen counter. Lights flashed across my eyes as I dropped to the ground with a loud thud. Nausea instantly washed over me, and I thought I was going to be sick. I could hear them both laughing, as I tried to roll to my side, but I couldn't move. I couldn't even think. My mind was in such a fog that I thought I'd heard Maverick's voice calling out to me, but I couldn't see him. I couldn't feel him. Everything was just black and the darkness consumed me.

Chapter 25

MAVERICK

"SHOOT THE BITCH, and let's get the hell out of here," a man shouted from Henley's apartment.

"I think we should have a little fun with her first," the other one laughed, and my blood ran cold. Their laughter fueled my rage, and I don't even remember kicking down her door. Henley was behind it, and I had to get to her. My mind was on auto pilot. I didn't even think before I kicked the door down, splintering it on its hinges.

Adrenaline soared through my body as I charged into the room with my brothers following close behind me. I stopped dead in my tracks when I saw Henley sprawled out on the floor with blood pooling around her head. My eyes shot to the man who was standing over Henley, and without hesitation, I aimed my gun at him. Our unexpected invasion caught him off guard, and he had little time to react. His eyes darted towards my gun, and panic washed over him as he watched me squeeze the trigger. The imminent dread he felt caused his body to tense as the bullet hit him directly between the eyes. Satisfaction washed over me as his lifeless body dropped to the ground.

I rushed over to Henley's side, dropping down to my knees, and I placed my fingers on her neck, praying that I could find a pulse. It was faint, but I could feel her heart beat lightly thumping against the tips of my fingers. Relief surged through me when I realized that she was still alive. My heart ached as I studied the bruises covering her face, and I wanted to beat that fucker with my bare hands and shoot him all over again.

I tried to pull my shit together as I turned to Cotton and said, "She's alive, but she's lost a lot of blood. We've got to get her to a hospital."

"I'll call the ambulance," Cotton snapped as he grabbed his phone from his pocket. Then he turned to Smokey and said, "You boys get this mess cleaned up before they get here."

"On it," Smokey told him as they quickly began disposing of the body.

Guardrail had managed to wrestle the other man to the ground, and quickly bound his hands behind his back with zip ties. When he was finished, Guardrail grabbed his arm, tugging him upright. He looked over to Cotton and said, "I'll get this one over to the club. Stitch is already getting things prepared for our guest." The guy could barely see as Guardrail led him out of the apartment, and I knew his night of hell had just begun. Stitch would have him wishing he was dead in a matter of minutes.

I took a cloth from the counter and gently pressed it against Henley's head. She was so still, almost lifeless. I was watching her slip away, and I couldn't stand the thought of losing her.

"Henley… baby, wake up," I pleaded, but I got no response. She didn't open her eyes. She didn't give me any sign that she was still with me. "I need you to wake up, Henley. You've got to *wake up*!"

Cotton walked over to me and placed his hand on my shoulder. "Maverick, you've got to keep it together, brother. She's going to need you when she comes around," he explained.

"Why did she do this? Why would she risk her life like this? It doesn't making any sense," I asked as I took her hand in mine.

"You know why she did it. She did it for you, brother. She did it for the Club. And she was able to accomplish something we haven't. Because of her, we might finally get some answers. She's one hell of a girl," Cotton said as he looked over to Henley. "She'll be alright, Maverick. She's a lot stronger than you think."

There was a knock on the front door, and the

room fell silent. Cotton glanced around one final time, before he let the medics in. They rushed over to Henley and one of them asked, "Can you tell us what happened?"

"There was a break-in. We don't know much more than that," Cotton explained. "We walked in and found her like this."

After checking all of her stats, they carefully lifted her up onto the gurney. They were about to take her down to the ambulance when I asked, "Is she going to be okay?"

"It's hard to say. She's suffered a blunt force trauma to the head. We won't know how serious it is until we get her over to the hospital." He continued to talk as he pushed her towards the elevator. "The doctors will probably do a CT Scan and maybe an MRI. That will tell them how severe the injury really is."

"I'm riding with her," I told him.

"Are you a relative?" he asked.

"Yes," I lied, but there was no way that I was going to leave her side.

"Okay, we've got room." The ambulance was waiting for us at the front door, and once they had her loaded up in the back, I crawled in behind them. When the doors slammed shut and the sirens roared above me, I had never been so terrified in my life. Looking at Henley so hurt and helpless, I felt lost. I felt powerless. I had no control as I watched the medics continue to work on her. Nothing before had ever frightened me like this. My heart ached when I thought about losing her. I loved her. I couldn't imagine my life without her. Her smile, the sound of her voice, the way she felt when I held her in my arms. I couldn't do it. I couldn't lose her.

When things finally settled down in the back of the ambulance, I asked again, "Is she going to be okay? You've got to give me something."

"Her vitals are improving, but I still don't know about her head injury. It could be a simple concussion, or something much more involved. We really won't know anything until we get the results from that CT scan," he explained.

While they carried Henley upstairs for testing, a nurse escorted me to the main waiting room. My brothers were already there waiting with Cassidy when I walked in. She came running towards me with tears streaming down her face. When she reached me, she wrapped her arms around my neck, hugging me tightly.

"I'm so sorry, Maverick. It wasn't supposed to happen like this. Henley promised that we'd have time to get away!" she cried hysterically.

"What the hell were you thinking, Cass? Henley's back there fighting for her life," I snapped.

"She was just so determined. She thought if she used herself as bait, you'd be able to catch the men that killed Skidrow," she explained as she wiped the tears from her face. Her story sounded too fucking familiar.

"Where did she get the idea? Had she been talking to anyone?" I asked.

"I'm not sure. Big Mike, maybe? But you know Henley. She's always coming up with these crazy ideas, but I thought this one might really work. She was just trying to help."

Fuck. I couldn't believe what I was hearing. Henley would've never gotten into this mess, if Mike had kept his goddamn mouth shut. Clenching my fists at my side, I glared at him, trying to fight the urge to kick his ass right here in the middle of the fucking waiting room. The blood drained from his face when he noticed me glaring at him. He took a step towards me, but I raised my hand, signaling him to stop. I had every intention of having it out with him, but this was not the place. He'd just have to wait.

I spent the next three hours feeling like I was coming apart at the seams while I waited to hear something from Henley's doctor. The walls were closing in on me. I paced back and forth, and my heart stopped beating every time a doctor or nurse walked by the doorway. It was obvious that I was on edge, so my brothers steered clear, giving me time to pull my shit together. I hated the waiting, not knowing what was going on with her. My imagination kept jumping to the worst-case scenarios, and they were driving me insane.

I was about to lose the last of my patience,

when a nurse called out, "I need to speak with someone from Miss Henley Gray's family."

Cassidy and I anxiously looked at each other before we walked towards the door. Time stood still as I waited for the nurse start talking.

"I just wanted to give you an update on Henley," the nurse started. "They just got the results back from the CT scan, and Henley does have a concussion and a laceration on the back of her head. They've moved her to a room at the end of the hall."

"How's she doing? Is she awake?" Cassidy asked with tears streaming down her cheeks.

"She's a little groggy, and she's going to have one hell of a headache. But she'll be just fine."

"When can we see her?" I asked. I was relieved to know that she was okay, but I needed to see it for myself. I had to know that she really was okay.

"She's been asking for someone named Maverick? I take it that's you," she said with a warming smile.

"Yes ma'am. I'm Maverick," I told her.

"Why don't you come with me? I still need to sort out her medication, but you can sit with her while I get it worked out," she said as she started up the hall.

I started to follow her when Cassidy grabbed my arm and said, "Tell her that I'm sorry," she wailed unable to control her tears.

I put my arms around her, pulling her close to me and said, "I'll come back to get you as soon as I can. Just hold tight until then." She nodded, and I gave her another tight squeeze before I let her go. She stood at the doorway, watching until I walked into Henley's room.

I was so anxious to see her that I didn't think before I rushed into her room. I didn't take the time to prepare for seeing her lying in that hospital bed. She was so fucking pale, making the bruises along her face seem even darker. There was a small bandage around her head, but even at her worst, she was beautiful. I couldn't stop staring at her. She was alive and lying just a few steps from me. My prayers had been answered. Her lips curved into a small smile when she noticed me standing at the end of her bed.

"Hey," she whispered.

"How are you feeling," I asked.

"I've been better," she confessed.

I nodded, crossed my arms, and continued to look at her as I thought about what I was going to do next. I wanted to hold her, to tell her that everything was going to be okay, but I couldn't. Not yet. She wouldn't be in this hospital bed if she'd just used her damn head.

"Aren't you going to say something? Yell... scream... fuss at me? Something?" she asked.

"Do you want me to tell you how a part of me died when I saw you lying on that floor, or how hard it was to sit out there for the past three fucking hours not knowing if you were going to live or die?" I asked.

"Maverick... I'm sorry. I know I screwed it all up," she explained.

"I thought I made it clear... I told you that I would tan your ass if you even *thought* about getting involved in club business. Do you remember that, Henley? I hope you do, because I am going to enjoy spanking that pretty little ass of yours when you get out of this hospital."

"What is it with you and my ass?" she asked with a giggle. "You need to stop teasing me. I'm injured."

"What can I say? I like your ass. Enough said. You'll get better, and I'll be waiting," I smirked. It was impossible for me to be angry with her right now. I had her back, and I wasn't about to waste one minute on bullshit that just didn't matter. She was out of danger, and she was going to be okay. Besides, I knew she'd learned her lesson. After tonight, there's no way she'd ever do something like this again.

Chapter 26

HENLEY

★

"**O**H MY GOD… Cassidy! Is she okay?" I asked frantically. My mind had been in such a fog, I'd forgotten that I hadn't seen her since that man grabbed me and dragged me up the fire escape.

"She's a little shaken up, but she's fine," Maverick explained.

"Thank god. I wouldn't be able to live with myself if anything had happened to her because of my hair brained idea."

"I'm pretty sure she won't be so quick to go along with you next time," he said smiling. I was relieved that he wasn't furious with me. This little exploit of mine put everyone in danger, and I wouldn't blame him for hating me right now. I couldn't help but wonder if I'd done it all for nothing.

"Can I ask you something?" I asked apprehensively.

"You can ask, but that doesn't mean I'll answer," Maverick snickered.

"Did you get them? Did you get the guy that killed Skidrow? He was there," I started. Just thinking about that man brought chills down my spine.

"You mean you recognized one of them?"

"Yes. He was there that night… I remembered his voice," I told him unable to stop my own from trembling.

"Are you sure it was him?" he asked.

"There's no doubt in my mind. I'll never be able to forget that man," I admitted. When I closed my eyes I could still see that large snake tattoo taunting me. "Please tell me… did you get him?" I asked again.

He walked over to me and reached for my hand, kissing the tips of my knuckles. "Yeah, baby. We got him."

"Did he tell you who he was? Why they killed Skidrow?" I prodded.

"Don't worry about all that, Henley. We'll get what we need out of him. You just concentrate on getting yourself out of this hospital," he said as he sat down on the edge of the bed.

"Thank you. Thank you for coming tonight… for saving my life," I whispered, unable to fight back my tears.

"Henley, you're mine. I know I haven't been clear about that. I've been too bull headed to admit it out loud, but I've known it since the night you were trying to leave the club wearing nothing but that damn t-shirt. I couldn't stand the thought of you walking out that door. No one has been able to get to me the way you do – no one. I love you, Henley," he said as he leaned over me, kissing me softly on my lips. In that moment, I knew I loved Maverick with every fiber of my being. He wasn't a man that gave away his love freely, and I was overwhelmed by the thought that he had given it to me.

"I love you, too, Logan. Now and forever," I told him. I leaned in to kiss him, and the moment his mouth met mine, I was lost. He was everything I'd ever wanted and more, and now he was mine.

We were still kissing when Cassidy eased into the room and said, "Sorry, I couldn't hold out any longer. I just needed to see for myself that you were okay." She was a mess. Her eyes were swollen from crying and mascara was running down her cheeks.

"It's okay, Cass. Really, I'm fine," I said trying to reassure her.

"Well, you look like shit," she said with a soft laugh.

"You look a hot mess yourself," I told her as I reached out my arms and gave her a hug. She started to cry again, so I held her close to my chest until she pulled herself together.

"I don't know why I let you talk me into do-ing these crazy things with you. You could have gotten yourself killed tonight. I was so scared, Lee Bug. I thought I had lost you," she whim-pered.

"You know, I blame you for all of this," I told her smiling. "You're supposed to be the smart one. You should've talked me out of it."

"Don't you start that shit with me! You know I didn't think we should do it," she said, her face turning red with frustration.

"They got him," I whispered.

"You mean it actually worked?"

I looked over to Maverick while I said, "It was stupid of us to get involved like that, and we will never do anything like that again, but yeah. It worked." I couldn't stop my mouth from curling into a huge grin.

"I'm still going to kick your ass for scaring me like that," Cassidy snickered.

"I can't say that I blame you."

"We need to let her get some rest," Maverick interrupted.

"I can stay with her tonight… help keep an eye on things," she offered.

"I'm staying. Go home and get some sleep. I'll call you in the morning to let you know how she's doing."

Cassidy hugged me once more and said, "I'll come check on you tomorrow. I love you, Sis."

"I love you, too." Cassidy was an amazing sister. She never failed to be there when I needed her, and I knew I was lucky to have her.

"I'm going to head out. Try to behave."

Chapter 27

MAVERICK

AFTER I GOT Henley settled in our room, I set out to find Stitch. No one had seen him since last night when Guardrail brought in the motherfucker that killed Skidrow. He'd been working on him in the warehouse for the past twenty-four hours, which let me know that Stitch was taking his time working this guy over. There was no telling what hell he'd put that man through, but I knew when it was all said and done, he'd have all the information we needed to get these guys once and for all.

"Have you been by to check on Stitch?" I asked Cotton. He was busy working in his office, and seemed surprised to see me.

"I thought you were still at the hospital. How's Henley?" he asked.

"She's doing better. They released her this morning, and now she's resting in my room," I explained. Until this morning, I hadn't really missed not having a place of my own, but now I was thinking it was time to start looking for a house. I wanted Henley to have a home that she could be proud of, one that was close to her school, so she could finish up her classes and graduate.

"Good. I'm glad she's doing better. I hate to admit it, but the girl saved our asses last night. We have our first real lead because of her."

"Should've never happened."

"True, but it did. That's on you, Maverick. You're the Sergeant of Arms for a reason. I expect you to keep this club safe. Make sure it doesn't happen again. You know I like Henley. I think she's a good woman and she's been good for you. But if she pulls a stunt like this again, there will be *consequences*," he warned.

"I'll see that she doesn't."

"I hope so. Now, let's go check on our boy. I want to see what he's been able to get out of our guest."

I followed Cotton to the back of the ware-house where Stitch had created his playroom. The overwhelming stench of death hit me as soon as we walked through the door, making my stomach churn from the smell. Stitch was sitting on an old, wooden stool in the corner of the room smoking a cigarette, and he didn't seem to notice that we had walked in.

"Stitch?" I called out to him. When he didn't

answer, I walked over to him, placing my hand on his shoulder and said, "How you making it, brother?"

"Making progress…" he mumbled. I didn't miss the glazed look in his eyes or his blood soaked shirt. He was exhausted, but wouldn't give up until he was certain that he had everything he could get out of him.

"What kind of progress?" Cotton asked.

"His name is Victor," he said, pointing to what was left of the man they brought in last night. When I caught sight of his mangled body, my gut tightened in rage thinking of what he'd just done to Henley. His wrists were bound in thick chains, and he was hanging from a rafter in the ceiling with blood dripping down around his feet. It looked like both his shoulders were dislocated as his head was hung low, his chin resting on his chest. He didn't look like he was still conscious, but even if he was, I wouldn't be able to tell from all the swelling on his face. Both of his eyes were completely swollen shut, and his face was covered in blood and bruises.

Stitched tossed his cigarette to the floor and lit another one as he said, "He's a member of the King Pythons' Syndicate. Their club is based out of Anchorage, Alaska, and they have over thirty-five members in their charter. They've developed a new kind of Meth. It's stronger… more addictive, and just like you thought, they're looking to expand their distribution," he confirmed. "They set their sights on Clallam County because of our port access."

"Did he say why they killed Skid?" I asked.

"He wouldn't give them information on the club, so they shot him," he growled.

"You think he's got anything left in him?" I asked as I looked over to Victor, and I couldn't tell if he was even breathing.

"I'll get another couple of hours out of him," Stitch told me with a sinister smile.

"We'll leave you to it," Cotton said as he started for the door. "Just let me know when you're done, and I'll get the boys to come help you take out the trash."

We were just about to walk out the door, when I took a bucket of cold water and emptied it over Victor's head. He groaned as he pulled against the chains, trying to free himself. I reached over to Stitch's torture table and grabbed the ammonia. "Wake up, sunshine. I'm not done with you yet."

"Please… I've told your man everything I know," Victor pleaded.

"We'll see about that." I replied, as I grabbed hold of his head and held it up, ensuring whatever faculties he had left, got what I had to say.

"You know this is your end Victor, right?" I screamed so close, speckles of my spit splattered across his face. "But what you don't know is how it's going to end. I want you to think of your brothers, your family... every person you have ever loved while you answer Stitch's questions, Victor. I want you to think about their end. Because right now, their lives are in your hands. Think about the children you left with no father while you're cooperating with Stitch. Consider this your last chance for redemption, Victor."

When I finally released him, his head plunged down to his chest. He was defeated, knowing what I said was true, and it was only a matter of time before he told us everything he knew. As I turned to leave, Stitch pulled his stool over next to him. He started talking to him so low that I couldn't understand what he was saying. The door slammed behind us as we headed back to the clubhouse. We walked in silence as we listened to Victor's tortuous screams.

When we reached the clubhouse, Cotton turned to me and said, "I'm calling the guys in for church. We need to get Big Mike working on this."

"I'll go get him. There's something I've been meaning to talk to him about," I told him as I opened the door to the clubhouse and headed towards Mike's room.

I knocked on his door and listened as he stalked across the room. It took him a minute to answer, but I was waiting for him when he opened the door. His eyes widened when he saw me standing there, and he opened his mouth to speak. But before he had a chance to say anything, my fist rammed into the side of his face, forcing his head to lurch back. Mike was a big dude. He could have easily fought back and won, but he knew he was in the wrong. He should've never spoken to Henley about club shit, and it could've have cost him a lot more than a blow to his thick head.

He took a minute to collect himself before he said, "I'm sorry, Maverick. I fucked up."

"If you fuck up like that again, I'll have your patch," I warned.

"Understood, brother. It won't happen again," he promised.

"Cotton is calling church. We've got news," I told him. "We're going to need you to gather up all the intel you can find on the King Pythons Syndicate in Anchorage, Alaska."

"Is that them? Are they the ones that killed Skidrow?"

"Yeah, but Cotton has more. We need to get over there before they start," I told him as I turned to leave.

By the time we showed up, everyone had found their place at the meeting table. Cotton told them everything Stitch had uncovered, and we discussed our next move. It would take some time, but if we played our cards right, this whole mess could be over soon.

Chapter 28

HENLEY

I T'S BEEN ALMOST a week since I got out of the hospital, and I was about to go insane. At first it was so endearing and romantic to have the man I loved looking after me. It meant so much that he put everything else aside to be there with me. It was absolutely *wonderful...* for about two days. Then, it started to drive me crazy. He was so attentive... too attentive. I was feeling better – so much better, and I didn't really need him under my feet every stinking second. My head didn't even hurt anymore, and the bruises on my face were almost gone. I was being an ass. He was there for me when I needed him, and it wasn't right for me to find him so... annoying. I just wanted him to get back to being Maverick, my Maverick. I couldn't even fix a cup of coffee without him coming over to scold me for being out of bed. It's driving me up the freaking wall. If he didn't stop all this nonsense, I was going to have to hurt him… seriously *hurt him*!

On top of all of his doting, he had a new obsession. He was determined to find us a house, and it was exciting… at first. I couldn't wait to find a place for us to start our lives together, but he'd become totally neurotic about it. He's constantly on my computer searching for new listings, looking for the perfect place for us to live. I honestly didn't care what house we chose. I just wanted to be with him, and nothing else really matters.

"What about that place on Glenwood Drive? You think four bedrooms will be big enough?" Maverick asked.

"Four bedrooms is plenty. There's only two of us, you know."

"For now," he said as he walked over and sat on the edge of the bed.

"Yeah, well, for now, it's *plenty big*," I snapped at him as I put my book down beside me and started to get off the bed.

"Where are you going?"

I let out an exasperated sigh and said, "I'm going to get some lunch. And, no. I don't need any help."

"So you're feeling better?" he asked as he closed the laptop.

"Yes. I'm fine, Maverick," I said as I stood in front of him with my arms crossed. "I'm not sore. I don't have a headache. Most of my bruises are gone. I think I'm going to live, so please just chill *out*," I told him sarcastically.

"So you're all better," he snickered.

"Yes!" I spouted off, but the minute I caught sight of the sexy smirk on his face, I knew I was in trouble.

"Is that right? I've been waiting to hear that," he mocked.

"*Maverick…*" I warned.

Mischief danced in his eyes as he took hold of my arm and pulled me down across his lap. "Do you know how hard it's been waiting on you hand and foot? You are not a good patient," he taunted as his hand whipped through the air and landed on my ass.

I squirmed in his lap, trying to wiggle out of his hold as I screeched, "Maverick! I can't believe you just did that!"

"Baby, I'm just getting started," he said as he gently ran his hand over my backside. "I wondered how long you were going to milk this whole thing. I never thought of you as such a faker," he teased.

"Milking it? Are you kidding me?" I shouted defensively, turning back to face him.

His eyes sparkled with lust as his hand lifted and then popped against my ass for the second time. "Faker!"

"Have you lost your mind?! Stop! That hurt!" I screamed, but my laughter didn't make me sound very convincing. He knew he wasn't really hurting me. His hand gently grazed over my butt, and I knew he was about to strike again. While his hand was in the air, I managed to twirl myself around, straddling my legs around his waist. I slipped my hands around his neck as I said, "You can stop now. Consider my punishment received."

"I don't know about that. I'm not sure that you've learned your lesson," he said smiling. Damn, I loved that sexy smile. I dropped my hands down to his shoulders as I slowly rocked my hips against the growing bulge in his jeans.

"It's been a week," I pleaded.

Seconds later, Maverick had me pinned to the bed with my back against the mattress and his knees at my sides. As he hovered over me, an intense look crossed his face. It was there, plain to see, his feelings for me written across his face. He stared at me in silence for just a moment before he said, "I love you, Henley Gray."

There's nothing better than having the one person that you love most in the world look at you the way he was looking at me and saying those words out loud. It made my world stand still… holding me in that moment, making me want to stay there locked in his arms forever. I never thought I'd find a love like this, and now that I have, I'll never let it go.

"I love you, Logan. More than you know," I

whispered. He lowered his mouth to mine, and kissed me, slow and gentle, showing me just how much he really meant the words he'd said to me.

He released my hands just long enough to ease my t-shirt over my head, then slowly began nipping and sucking along the length of my neck as I tried to unbuckle his jeans. He lifted his hips as I slid them down his thighs. When they reached his ankles, he kicked them to the side of the bed. His fingers slipped into the sides of my cotton shorts, and quickly tugged them down my legs. He hovered over me, the warmth of his body fueling my need for him, and I could see that he wanted this just as much as I did. Unable to wait a minute longer, I reached down, gently taking his cock in my hand, and guided him inside of me. A low groan vibrated through his chest as he thrust deeply inside me, filling me completely as I cried out in pleasure.

I rocked my hips against his, enjoying the feeling of having him inside of me again, as I dragged my nails across his back. He withdrew a little, and then thrust back inside again and again, harder and faster with each stroke. I gasped with each retreat, eagerly awaiting his next invasion. The sounds of our bodies colliding filled the room as he quickened his pace.

"Oh god, Logan, you feel so good," I gasped as his relentless rhythm ignited a desire inside of me that would never go away. I lifted my ass, meeting every thrust of his hips, as the muscles in my abdomen began to tighten. My orgasm was slowly building, making my body quiver beneath him.

He lowered his face to mine and whispered, "That's it, baby. Don't hold back," before his lips crashed down against mine. My fingers dug into his hips as my climax took over, making it impossible for me to move. He continued to grind his hips against me as I clamped down around him forcing him to chase his own release. A deep growl shook through his chest, and with one final thrust, he came inside me. With a cocky grin on his face, he held himself over me, hovering between my legs as he stayed planted deep inside me.

His warm hands slid across my shoulders, soothing me as I tried to catch my breath. I inhaled deeply as a satisfied smile slowly crept across my face. I looked up to him and said, "You can punish me like that anytime."

Chapter 29

MAVERICK

Three months later

I PULLED MY bike behind Cotton and waited for Dallas to get Dusty's helmet on. The loud rumble of motorcycle engines surrounded me as I looked around the town square. I was amazed at the crowd that showed up for the event. There were over six hundred people lining the streets and another two hundred on bikes. I never expected to have such a huge turn out when I suggested having a charity run for children with Down's syndrome. I had gotten the idea when Dallas started having issues with her insurance company and mentioned how quickly Dusty's medical bills were adding up. I thought this might be a way to help her, and other families with children like Dusty, but I never imagined it would turn into something this big.

The run would last about six hours, and I planned to take Dusty along with me. I knew he wouldn't be able to make the entire trip, but I wanted him to have the chance to see some of this for himself. He was the main reason we decided to do this, so he should be here to enjoy it. Dallas finally had him ready to go, and he was busting with excitement. His little eyes sparkled with eagerness as he looked around at all the people, but Dallas was determined to get all of her rules in before she released him to me. She was going over all of her last minute warnings when I noticed Henley standing in the crowd. She was now wearing my name on her back, and she stood there smiling as her hands rested on her small round belly. I couldn't take my eyes off of her. She was everything to me and in that moment, everything became clear to me... it was right there all along. I got off my bike and she smiled at me as I walked over to her.

"I finally see it."

"What?" she asked.

I laid my hand on her pregnant belly and said, "I finally see my silver lining."

The End

Excerpt of Summer Storm after Acknowledgements

Dusty was just a character in a book, but the struggles he faces are real. There are so many excellent programs available to children and adults with Down's syndrome, but I wanted to let you know about a wonderful center that is located in my area. CS Patterson Training Center provides services for children and adults with a variety of challenges, and helps families learn to cope with the obstacles they may face. The CS Patterson Training Center provides access to group homes and employment opportunities for adults and early intervention for children. They work hard to provide their clients with a sense of independence, and people in the community have been great to support them. Unfortunately, each year the state has their typical cutbacks, and the center has faced some financial struggles. They do so much to help, and it would be awesome if you would check out their webpage. Thanks so much.

CS Patterson Training Center:
www.pattersontrainingcenter.com

Acknowledgements

Followed by an excerpt of Summer Storm

I would first like to thank my mother for all of her help and support with my writing. I wouldn't have been able to do any of this without her. Thank you for being such an awesome mom.

I would also like to give a special thank you to my new PA, Amanda Faulkner. I've heard authors brag about their PA's, but I really had no idea what I was missing until I met Amanda. She's always one step ahead of me, and I don't know how I ever made it without her. Posts, teasers, blogs…. It never ends. Thank you so much, Amanda!!

Marci Ponce is awesome! I truly wouldn't know what to do without her. She continues to push me as a writer and accepts nothing but the best with each and every book. Thank you so much for always being there and sharing your talent with me. You are truly an MC guru!

Danielle Deraney Palumbo is a true life saver. There are just no words to describe how thankful I am that you agreed to take the time to help me with Maverick's book. With everything that you have going on, you still managed to find the time to help me. Thank you so much. You are amazing!

I would also like to thank all of my readers. I have loved all of your comments and posts. I am floored every time I see one of your comments about liking my books. You have all been so supportive, and your comments always leave a smile on my face. When my life gets a little crazy, your kind words have given me the encouragement I've needed to continue on.

My Wilder's Women Street Team is amazing! Thank you all for your support. It means so much to me that you continue to help me with reviews and posting all of my teasers. Elizabeth Thiele, Neringa Neringiukas, Dawn Bryant, Mary Orr, and Rosetta Wagers are such a huge help to me. I am always amazed each time I see one of my teasers or my links that they have shared. Thank you for taking your time to help me. It means more than you will ever know.

I have been very blessed to have so much support from such a great group of women.

Sue Banner, Erin Osborn, Patricia Ann Blevins, Sherri Crowder, RB Hilliard, Keeana Porter, Terra Oenning, Danielle Palumbo, Kimberely Beale, Michelle Modesitte, Cora Brent, Trish Hash, Paula Rae, Jennifer Davidson, Michele Presley, Stephanie Page Sager, Lisa Menn Siegler, Race Crespin, and Brandy Kennedy, you guys never fail to make me smile with your amazing reviews and kind words!! Thanks so much for taking the time to read my books. Your reviews and comments mean so much to me!!

I want to give a special thank you to Monica Langley Holloway for all your help with creating my teasers and banners. You are so creative, and I truly appreciate you taking the time to help me.

Jordan Marie, you're an amazing author and friend. Thank you for all of your encouragement! You're always there with that extra little push that I needed to see me through. If you haven't had a chance to check out her new book, Claiming Crusher, then you are missing out. Go grab it!

Ana Rosso, my dear friend, I hope you have enjoyed this book. Even though you are hundreds of miles away, you are like my personal cheerleader. I hope Maverick lived up to all of your expectations. You are such a wonderful friend!!! Keep on rocking chickeroo!!

SUMMER STORM

A Satan's Fury MC Romance Series

Summer Storm
A Satan's Fury MC Romance Series
Copyright © 2015 L Wilder

Cover by: Carrie at cheekycovers.com

MAVERICK

There are things that happen in our lives that mark us forever. That change us in ways that we don't even understand. One chance meeting and fate casts her irrevocable spell. They say what doesn't kill you only makes you stronger, and that God doesn't give you more than you can handle. Unfortunately, those are just words, and they don't change shit.

I thought I had a good life, one I could be proud to call my own. My club meant the world to me, and I was proud to have them as my family. I knew I could depend on my brothers, and honestly they were really all I'd ever needed…. until I met Hailey. She was beautiful, smart, and sexy as hell. The woman captivated me…. Then she ripped my beating heart from my chest.

The hurt she caused cut me to the core. Her web of lies had had a catastrophic effect on my life and everyone else's she had come in contact with, but she wasn't around to see it. She wasn't around to see how her choices had affected so many people. No… she was gone. Gone from all of our lives forever, leaving me and mine and everyone that loved her in her wake, picking up the pieces of her betrayal.

This is my brother Guardrail's story. As VP, he was the one chosen to rectify the damage Hailey and her deceit had caused the club. He thought it would be simple – find the culprits and deal with them accordingly. He wasn't prepared for the storm that ensued… none of us were.

Chapter 1

ALLISON

"PARKER, ANY LEADS on a contractor yet?" My boss asked gruffly as he leaned against the doorway of my office.

I jumped in surprise, torn from my wayward thoughts and flustered by the sudden unwelcome intrusion.

"I have several I'm looking into now, actually," I replied with feigned confidence. It wasn't entirely true; I had really only focused on one.

"Well… let's get a move on it. The plans should've been finalized weeks ago," he said with a heavy sigh. I could tell he was guarding his words to hide his frustration. Normally it drove me nuts when Neil micromanaged me, but this time even I had to admit he had good reason. He had finally agreed to let me take the lead on a major project, and I had lost my focus. It was so unlike me. I normally got totally lost in my assignments. It was always so liberating. I loved putting my all into a worthy cause, and I had finally gotten the perfect opportunity to do just that.

"I need to have a full proposal with your chosen contractor by the end of the week," he asserted. He was done being polite, and I knew I'd be in hot water if it wasn't done on time.

"It will be ready, Mr. Yates. You know I wouldn't let the kids down."

"I know. I know. I'm just ready to get things started. Thanks for everything you do, Ms. Parker," he said as he walked out of my office. My mind started reeling as reality set in. The project was my chance to make a real difference. I needed to stop acting like a foolish teenager and pull my shit together. I couldn't afford to screw it up.

I knew firsthand how difficult being raised in the foster system could be. After my parents died when I was six, my older brother and I were put into foster care. Unfortunately, we were separated, and our foster families couldn't have been more different. Tony was placed with a family that already included four other foster kids, and their backgrounds were nothing like ours. He was surrounded by troubled teens and rebellion during his most formative years. Sadly, it became difficult for us to keep in contact as the turmoil took its toll and engulfed his home life.

My foster life wasn't filled with chaos and anarchy, though. Mine was… lonely. I was placed with a kind couple named Tom and Wendy who hadn't been able to have children of their own. They were nice, but not nice enough to take on my brother. In the beginning, after relentless pleading, they let him visit on several occasions, giving me vague hopes we could be reunited. When that didn't happen, I pulled away from their love. I didn't want a new family. I had a family, and I wanted them back.

I wasn't willing to just give up on being with my brother. He was too important to me. Through the years, I'd done everything in my power to keep in touch with him, but things changed and he started pulling away. He was always keeping secrets from me, and it worried me. I could see the angst in his eyes, but he wouldn't talk about it. When I asked him why he was pushing me away, he told me it was for my own protection. I tried to understand why he was doing it, but it still hurt. There was nothing I could do to help him, but there was no way I was going to lose him completely. Even if I didn't get to see him very often, I made sure to keep in touch through emails and phone calls, reminding him every chance I got that I would always be there for him.

Being without him, I retreated into myself and spent most of my time alone growing up. It wasn't until I started visiting the local community center that I finally started coming out of my shell. I met some of the other foster kids in town, and we created our very own sanctuary there. We would meet to hang out and play basketball or talk through things if we were in a tough spot. It was a place where we felt safe. We didn't feel judged or inadequate. We weren't outsiders there. We belonged.

That community center helped me learn how to deal with my anger and pain and turn it into something positive. Watching the older kids mentor the younger children helped me realize what I wanted to do with my life. I'd been working with the foster care system for the past eight years, and I'd devoted my life to making things better for those kids. Ever since I could remember, I'd wanted to find a way to make a difference, and I thought building a Youth Center would be a great way to help. I knew how much the community center where I had grown up had affected me, and it was important to me to make sure that these local kids had that support, too.

The center had to provide a stimulating environment for kids of all ages. I knew it needed to have a wide range of programs, activities, camps, and special events for the kids throughout the year. They needed to have a place to feel safe and spend time with their friends. It had taken a lot of work and fundraising, but I'd finally gotten it approved. Our Downtown Youth Center would have classrooms, a fitness center, a large auditorium, and a gymnasium with basketball courts. We would be able to offer activities and classes for the kids and their foster parents. I'd worked hard to make this project a possibility, and I wanted it to be perfect.

Once I had completed all the details, I placed several ads with all of our specs and projected budget. I encouraged any contractors that might be interested to contact me about submitting their bids, and the inquiries quickly began to fill my inbox. After reading through several offers, one in particular caught my attention. I wasn't sure what made his email stand out, but something pulled me to ask him for more information.

He and I spent the next few hours emailing back and forth. At first, the emails primarily consisted of contractor inquires and references, but then they grew increasingly more personal. I even found myself wondering if he was flirting with me a little. He was charming and funny, and I admit, I loved the attention. My imagination ran wild with possibilities of what the rugged, charismatic construction worker might have looked like. With every email, my mind tried to piece together my fantasy man. Our little online routine progressed just like that for several days. I still continued to look into the other offers, but his remained at the top of my list. After all, he had great references, and his proposal was below the budget. And… okay, there was something about seeing his name in my inbox that always made my heart skip a beat. I just couldn't resist.

I had gotten completely wrapped up in the fantasy, and I just didn't know what I was thinking. The Youth Center had been my dream for so long, but suddenly the charming stranger had taken over my every thought. He was like a drug, each message leaving me craving more. I found myself compulsively checking my inbox, looking for my fix. He had me hooked. Over the next week, the number of messages increased as the conversations became more addictive. I knew I should've stopped messaging him. He was a potential employee, and no good could come from it. But I couldn't stop myself. The truth was… I didn't want to.

It was easy to get lost in the fascination of some mysterious man, but it was more than that. I felt like I was getting to know him through his emails. His interest… his hobbies… even what he wanted in the future. This Kane Blackwood was no simple man. He was passionate about his work, and he was proud of the success he'd had at SF Construction. Kane was not afraid of hard work. It was one of the things I found most endearing about him. When he told me that he was a member of a motorcycle club, I was immediately intrigued. There was something about that secret world that I found appealing. As crazy as it sounded, the idea of having a group of brothers that had your back, of having a family that you could always turn to, made me envy him. When he first mentioned his motorcycle, I found myself fantasizing about what it would be like to ride with him. I had never been on one before, but the thought of it excited me, giving me goosebumps all over. Everything about him excited me, and truthfully, that scared me a little. The more we talked the more he seemed to be genuinely interested in me. That made me feel... well... wanted.

Honestly, the whole thing was the ideal situation for me. I'd always kept men at an arm's length, even if I really liked them. It was an unfortunate side effect from my solitary childhood. I didn't let my guard down easily, so romantic relationships had always been a struggle. My little online infatuation was the perfect mix of intimacy and self-preservation. I got the affection I craved without the danger of having to be truly vulnerable. The anonymity of being online gave me the safety net I needed to be confident and flirty... brazen even. I allowed myself to open up for the first time in forever and engage in a little harmless fun. He had a way with words, and it was hot. I didn't want it to end.

We continued down that path for almost two weeks, messaging back and forth every chance we got. As Neil started to remind me of our deadlines, though, I began to get nervous. I was going to have to actually meet Kane soon and get the ball rolling on the Youth Center. No more hiding behind my computer. I had to show him the location of the building site, and I needed to discuss the blueprints with him.

Neil had started prowling around just outside of my office, glancing in my direction like he knew something was going on. I shook my head and tried to focus on the task at hand. I pulled up my email, and after explaining Neil's demands, I asked Kane if he could meet me at the site on Thursday. I had to get things started and fast. Time was up. As soon as I hit send, my heart started to race. What if I had been wrong about everything? What if he was some kind of serial killer? Or a fat, balding old man with a boner for younger women? I had been so stupid, but there was no turning back. I had no plan B. When his response popped up on my computer screen, however, all my doubts quickly disappeared.

May 1, 2015
2:45 p.m.
Kane Blackwood
SF Construction

Morning All-Star,

So Thursday's my lucky day, huh? Just tell me where and when, and I'm in. Don't

worry about your presentation. I'll make sure I'm ready; you just make sure _you're_ ready. I'm going to need you all day to get this done right.

BUTTERFLIES AND FEAR raced through me as I read his words. I smiled to myself when I saw the new nickname he had for me. I still don't know what had possessed me to tell him that silly story. I'd nearly died of embarrassment the day I tried my hand at baseball. I never forgot the expression on the coach's face as my ball crashed through the front windshield of his car. He was furious. It didn't matter that I had actually hit the ball for the first time; he was too busy freaking out about his car. I never was able to hit the ball like that again, and eventually I gave it up altogether. Sports were just not my thing.

Chapter 2

GUARDRAIL

"How's our little project going? Have you found out anything we can use?" Maverick asked.

"I know she isn't frightened of the club life like she should be, if that's any indication of how much she talks to her brother," I told him as I took a drink of my beer.

"You think she has any idea what he's been up to?" he asked.

"No. Nothing has come up on any of the feeds. He hasn't been to her house, and there hasn't been any communication between them through her phone or email. The prospects are still rotating shifts, and none of them have seen any sign of him."

As Vice President of Satan's Fury, it was up to me to find Tony, the lowlife motherfucker that stole a fifty thousand dollar shipment from the club. Because he'd been a long-standing leader of one of the street gangs in town, he'd gotten a unanimous vote at the table for the drug distribution. He was a professional, but in the end, he'd decided he could fuck us on our money. Surprisingly, the asshole actually thought he'd be able to get away with it.

He'd forgotten that Satan's Fury owned the whole damn town. Because drugs were an unavoidable reality in the outer east and west side of our territory, we negotiated which gangs could run product and where. It was the best way for us to keep control of what drugs were sold in our area. We'd allowed Tony and his minions to distribute our product, same as the other little set on the west side. We used them out of necessity. Our product kept us in control of the territory. They did the distribution, and we took our cut... a large cut.

Nobody in the clubhouse talked to anyone about anything, so we were caught off guard when Tony managed to manipulate Maverick's girl, Hailey, to get information about the club. It cut deep. Maverick had it bad for Hailey, and no matter how many times she'd come and gone, he was always there for her. Hell, he didn't even realize she'd gotten hooked on junk until it got bad, and even after that it took an overdose for him to finally be able to cut her off. Although we all knew he would never share club business, the whole situation had us all on edge.

The last time she called Maverick begging for money, he'd tried putting her off by telling her he was going on a run and wouldn't be back for a week. Unfortunately, Hailey's decision to give Tony that little tidbit of information had given him a five-day jump that nobody saw coming, and it had cost us… big. We'd come home early only to find that Tony and his crew had taken off with our money, and Hailey was nowhere to be found. It was a shit ton of fuckery.

They had to be found… all of them. We knew Tony was hiding, and we had eyes everywhere. It was only a matter of time before we found him. We started with their families. Unfortunately, none of them kept any strong family ties that we could pull intel from. They had kids like kittens, and too many baby's mamas to count. Since we decided that cutting the head off the snake was our best option, Maverick, our Sergeant of Arms, and I have spent weeks searching for information on Tony's whereabouts. When we came across the name of his sister, we both agreed she was our best lead.

"Has she said anything about Tony? Do you think she knows where he is?" Maverick asked.

"Nothing yet, but she's opening up more every day. If she does know anything or he contacts her, I'll get her to talk," I told him confidently. I could tell she was beginning to trust me. A part of me felt guilty about misleading her, but in the end, I knew I didn't have a choice.

"You'll find him. Once you put your mind to something, there's no stopping you," Maverick told me as his hand slapped against my back. "That's why the Pres put you on this."

"I'll do whatever it takes to find him, and he'll pay for fucking with the club," I told him as I slammed my empty beer bottle down on the counter. "He will slip up, and I'll be there waiting when he does."

From what I could tell, Allie hadn't spent a lot of time with her brother recently. They'd both been in the foster care system, but growing up in separate homes had made them completely different people. She'd made a life for herself, while Tony fell deep into drugs, alcohol, and gang life. I'd been able to retrieve several emails he'd sent her over the past few years. It was obvious that Tony did what he could to keep his sister from his lifestyle, but whenever he got down on his luck, she was always the first one he'd reach out to. She always remained loyal to him. Even when she knew his life was spinning out of control, she was there when he tried to contact her. Her love for her brother never wavered, and I respected her for that.

He'd royally fucked up this time, and something in my gut told me that he'd try to contact her. Just like he always had, he'd come running to her when the shit hit the fan. I needed to get in contact with her, so when I saw the ad in the paper, I knew I had my in. I'd known that she worked for Child Services, but I didn't realize that she was so invested in making things better for those kids. I had to admit, I liked that about her. It was one thing to work with them every day, but this was more than an ordinary house visit. This would help a lot of kids all at once, and she'd come up with the entire plan herself.

"If she knows something, you'll get it out of her," Maverick told me with confidence. "Just be patient."

"Yeah, but it may be harder than I thought."

"Why's that?"

"It's... I don't know, man. She's just not what I expected," I confessed. "Hell, I don't know how to explain it."

"I get it, brother. I've seen her picture. She's a hot ass. I can see why you might get a little distracted," he snickered.

"It's not that. She's just... different," I told him. "I thought she'd be some kind of stuck up bitch. Hell, you've seen her... all dressed up in that fancy shit, business suits and high heels. I wasn't expecting her to be so... whatever. It doesn't matter. If she knows something about Tony, I'll get it out of her."

"Ha, wait a minute... sounds like she's getting to you, brother," Maverick prodded.

"Maybe, but it's just a job. Finding out where that dickhead ran off to is my only focus," I told him, but I knew it wasn't that easy. I was a selfish bastard, and I wanted it all. Ultimately, I knew I had to deal with Tony, but Allie definitely had me thinking. I found myself in an impossible situation, and I had no idea if I could make it work.

"Whatever you say, man. Just be careful with all that. Remember, her brother is walking dead… nothing is going to change that. If you need any help, you know where to find me," Maverick offered.

Maverick was a good man, one you could depend on. Unfortunately, he had a hard time believing that. He was still carrying around a lot of guilt from the shit that'd gone down over the past few months, but he never let that get in the way of the club. He was a brother that you could always depend on.

"Thanks, man," I responded.

"Hey, you never know… maybe this thing with her will work out. I've seen crazier things happen."

"Good things like her don't happen to me, brother," I told him, shaking my head. He patted my back as he turned to leave. As I watched him walk out of the bar, my mind drifted back to Allie. I found myself wondering if Maverick could be right. Was there a way that I could actually have her? Without thinking, I pulled out my phone to see if she had responded to my last email. I couldn't stop the smile that spread across my face when I saw her name.

> **May 1, 2015**
> **3:15**
> **Allison Parker**
> **Department of Children's Services**
>
> **All-Star?? Really? You're going to pay for that one, mister. :)**
>
> **Looking forward to Thursday. I'll bring the coffee.**

THE GIRL WAS getting to me. I knew that she was becoming a real distraction, and I needed to focus on her lowlife brother. There was one problem though… I couldn't stop my finger from hitting the reply button.

> **May 1, 2015**
> **3:30**
> **Kane Blackwood**
> **SF Construction**
>
> **I'll take mine however you like yours, All-Star.**
>
> **See you Thursday.**

May 1, 2015
4:25
Allison Parker
Department of Children's Services

How do you do that? You give me a crazy nickname, and I'm sitting here smiling like a goof. I think you're getting to me.

BTW, thanks for the "coffee order." :)

Chapter 3

ALLIE

WHEN I WALKED into the office, everyone was standing around grumbling as they drank their morning cup of coffee. I smiled and tried not to act too eager about getting back to my office. I wanted to check my email. I hadn't been online since yesterday afternoon, and I was curious to see if Kane had messaged me back.

As soon as I sat down at my desk, I saw that I had a message in my inbox. I anxiously clicked the button to open my emails, and his name was the first one that caught my attention.

May 2, 2015
9:45 p.m.
Kane Blackwood
SF Construction
Like that I'm getting to you, babe.
Night.

May 3, 2015
9:08 a.m.
Allison Parker
Department of Children's Services

Morning, :)

Hope you're having a good day. I've been thinking about you. Wondering if you're as good with your hands as you say you are....

JUST AS I was about to click the send button, Neil walked into my office, interrupting my train of thought. "Daniel sent over the changes to the blueprints this morning. Have you had a chance to look them over?"

"I was just about to ask you about that. Do we really have to take out the meeting room?" I asked with a sad sigh.

"Allie, it's just not in the budget. If you can find a way to fund it, then you can have him put it back in the plan," Neil said as he leaned against my doorframe. His arms were crossed and resting on his protruding belly. I had to fight the urge to roll my eyes at him.

"Maybe we could reduce the size of the fitness center," I suggested.

"We've already made that deal with Health and Fitness Retro. We can't risk losing their sponsorship."

"You're right. I just hate to see things get taken away. We've worked so hard. I want everything to be perfect."

"Focus on finalizing the bids. I want to have it on my desk by Friday afternoon. I need to check everything over before the board sees it on Monday," Neil told me.

"I'm meeting the contractor on Thursday."

"Be ready to present any new ideas to them on Monday. They're eager to hear what you've been working on."

"I'll have everything ready," I promised.

He nodded and stepped into the hall. "Looking forward to it," he called back.

I turned back to my computer and started to gather my files.

May 3, 2015
12:25 p.m.
Kane Blackwood
SF Construction

Are you questioning my abilities, All-Star?

May 3, 2015
1:10 p.m.
Allison Parker
Department of Children's Services

I know better than that.

May 3, 2015
1:15 p.m.
Allison Parker
Department of Children's Services

Anyway, Mr. Confident,

I am actually looking forward to seeing you live up to this reputation of yours. :)

May 3, 2015
1:35 p.m.
Kane Blackwood
SF Construction

Ms. Curiosity,

I will. Don't you worry about that, sweetheart.

I WAS TRYING to think of a flirty response to Kane's last email when a text message from my brother popped up on my phone. My heart dropped. I hadn't heard from him in weeks and seeing a phone number I didn't recognize really made me start to worry. There had to be something wrong. There was a time that I'd thought Tony was the best brother in the world. I'd looked up to him and thought he would always be there to protect me. In his defense, I think he tried. I knew a part of him worried about me, but his life had taken a different turn than mine. He didn't want me involved in the things he was dealing with, so he pulled away from me… only sending text messages or emails to keep in touch. I hated it. He was the only family I had left, and he chose drugs and money over me. It hurt.

Need to talk to you. It's important.

T

WELL, SHIT. THAT didn't sound good. I had to wonder if he was in some kind of trouble. The last time we talked, I could tell that he was upset about something. He wouldn't tell me what was going on, but I could see the concern in his eyes. I didn't think twice about confirming that I would be there. He was the only family I had left. I had to help him if he needed it.

Chapter 4

GUARDRAIL

"NEED TO KNOW where we are with Tony," Cotton told me. As club president, he ruled with an iron fist. When he gave an order, he expected results... immediate results, and I had nothing. He was depending on me to deal with Tony, and I could tell he was getting restless.

"Meeting the sister today," I told him assertively. "I've got this, Pres."

"We've got to make an example of him, Kane. No one fucks with the club... no one." The deep crow's feet around his dark eyes crinkled as anger crept over his face.

"He'll slip up, and when he does, I'll be there. You can count on that," I told him, trying to reassure him.

He tugged thoughtfully at the ends of his long white goatee as he said, "What about this Youth Center? You really going to try for that with everything that's going on?"

When Cotton came up with the club starting its own construction company, I was intrigued. He wanted a cover for the money we were bringing in from early distribution, and we both agreed that a company like this would be the perfect front. I had no idea if we'd be able to pull it off, but I wanted to give it a try. I'd always had a passion for building things, and I was good at it. At first, we built small houses, trying to build a name for ourselves. It didn't take long for us to become one of the best companies in the city. Our work was good, and we submitted the best bids to ensure our growth. Everyone came to us, and we were constantly expanding. It truly was a perfect cover. Not only did it launder money for the club, it provided all the patches working there viable proof of income as well.

"It's one of the biggest projects we've had in a while. If they accept the bid, it could be a real good opportunity for us… opening doors down the road," I told him.

"I get that, but this whole thing could get messy. It's not about getting the job. She could find out that you're looking for her brother, and that would have consequences. Just play it safe," he ordered.

I nodded and walked out of his office. There was no point in arguing with him. I knew he was right. This wasn't about some fucking construction project. It was about finding Tony. I had to make myself remember that.

I headed down the hallway to my room. I wanted to get changed before I met up with Allie. I threw on a pair of jeans and a plaid button-down shirt, trying to play the part of the contractor she would be expecting. Before I left, I went by the office to pick up everything I might need for my meeting with her. I wanted to get to the site early, so I could look over things one last time to check my figures. I knew it was crazy, but I wanted to get the bid for my own selfish reasons. I'd pretty much left her fucked with no time for other options, and truthfully, now I wanted more time with her regardless of if it got us Tony.

I was leaning against my truck when she pulled into the parking lot. I patiently waited as she fumbled around inside the car. Then, she finally opened the door and stepped out. As soon as her high heels hit the pavement, my eyes followed the line of her long, slender legs up to her thighs where her skirt had hiked up a little during her drive. The curls of her long, brown hair flowed down around her shoulders, concealing her face as she looked down to adjust her short, gray skirt. Damn. That sexy ass skirt hugged her curves in all the right places, bringing my cock to life right in the fucking parking lot. She quickly pulled her hair to the side and looked over to me. Her beautiful, pouty lips slowly curved into a sexy smile as her dark brown eyes met with mine. At that moment, all my thoughts of Tony were instantly forgotten. He became a distant memory as my entire mind was devoured by the beauty standing before me.

"Hey there, handsome," she said. Just the sound of her voice made the world stop turning on its axis. I couldn't explain it. It was like she had cast a spell on me, and I was unable to resist it. I wanted her. Hell, just seeing her standing there made me think about the future. I'm not that kind of man… I had never thought about my future… not with anyone, but now suddenly I was envisioning bike rides, a white picket fence… even rug-rats running around. It didn't make any fucking sense. I watched as she started walking towards me, her hips casually swaying from side to side. Her gorgeous smile never wavered as she approached me. Perfect… she was fucking perfect.

"Looking good, All-Star." A light blush of red crossed her cheeks as she tucked her hair behind her ear. Beautiful.

"Always the charmer," she said as she handed me a cup of coffee. "You definitely know how to make a girl smile."

"I can think of more than a few ways I'd like to bring a smile to that beautiful face," I told her and grinned as I saw the curiosity flicker in her eyes. I stepped closer, and her breath stopped, only confirming what I already knew. She was into me. The sexual energy was raging between us immediately. I fucking loved it.

"You're quite the flirt, Mr. Blackwood."

I leaned down, just inches from her ear, and whispered, "Just stating the facts, sweetheart." She shifted her feet and awkwardly fumbled with the lid on her coffee cup. I loved watching her try to hide her body's reaction to me, but it was useless. I could tell that I was getting to her. "And call me Kane."

"Okay… Kane," she said with a bashful smile, looking down at her coffee cup.

"Don't get shy on me now, darling," I told her as I inched closer to her. We had shared so much over the past few weeks in our messages, I felt like I truly knew her.

She tilted her head as she looked up to me with wonder. She slowly lifted her hand up to my face and placed the palm of her hand on my cheek. "Are you really here? Is this really happening?"

"Yeah, Allie. It is," I told her.

"I thought I had made it all up in my head," she said with a light chuckle.

"Allie."

"I was worried that you might be some kind of creeper."

"No one said that I wasn't," I said, laughing.

"Or bald."

I couldn't hold back my laugh, "No… I'm not bald."

"I can't believe it. I never thought I could get to know someone… to have feelings for someone without actually meeting them first. I feel like…."

"I know, Allie. I know exactly what you mean." I leaned down and pressed my lips against hers, immediately feeling my body come alive in a way it never had before. Her touch set me on fire. The intensity was almost too much, but I couldn't pull away. I needed more. My hands reached for her hips, pulling her body into mine as she opened her mouth to me… warm and wet. Fuck. She was every man's fantasy… my fantasy. Mine. A light moan vibrated through her chest, urging me on as I deepened the kiss, claiming her mouth with mine. Her fingers tangled in my hair, forcing a growl to escape through my lips. I wanted her… all of her. A thousand thoughts raced through my mind as I stood there holding her close to me.

She was everything… everything I could never have. Suddenly, my heart felt like it was clamped in a vise. What the fuck was I thinking? Our club was going to kill her brother. He was the only family she had left, and we were going to take him from her. Damn. I knew better than this. I knew she'd never be able to forgive me.

We were destined to be destroyed. I pulled back and looked down at her. Her lips were full, damn near bruised from our kiss and begging to be kissed again. I took a deep breath and did my best to rein in my need for her. I couldn't let it happen. Not then… not like that.

"Kane?" she asked. Her face was marked with confusion as she looked up at me. "Is something wrong?"

"No, Allie," I told her as I stepped away from her. As hard as it was, I knew that I had to stop. I couldn't lead her to believe that there could be something between us, when I knew what the end would be. I didn't want to hurt her, but there wasn't any way around it. "We… um, we just need to talk about the specs."

"I…. Sure. I wasn't thinking," she said as she took a step back.

"I've already had my guys survey the area, so I just need to know if there have been any changes since we talked last night," I told her, trying to sound professional.

"No, everything is all set. Neil wants to review the final quote before we present it to the board on Monday. Do you think you could give it to me by tomorrow?" she asked nervously.

"Allie…do you trust me?" Her face filled with anxiety, and it gutted me. "I'll have it. I told you not to worry. I've already done most of the work. I'm pretty close to wrapping it up."

"Really? Are you sure?" she asked excitedly.

"I'm sure. I'll send it over to you tonight," I told her. She was just about to say something else when her phone rang. She reached into her side pocket and pulled out her phone. I could see the worry in her eyes the moment that she read the message. Her hands trembled as she stared at her phone.

"Allie? What is it? What's wrong?" I asked.

"It's nothing. It's just my brother. He needs to see me about something," she said, sounding a little nervous.

"You look upset. Are you okay?" I asked as I reached out and ran my hand down her quivering arm, trying to comfort her.

"Yeah... yeah, I'm fine. He just wants to meet up," she said as she fiddled with the buttons on her phone.

"When? Do you need to leave now?"

"No, no. We're meeting at Lancaster's on Sunday at 7:00," she said with a heavy sigh. "I'm just worried that he's gotten himself into some kind of trouble again," she mumbled, thinking out loud.

"Don't worry about it. It's not a big deal. Everything will be fine," she continued, but I could see the apprehension in her eyes. I didn't like it... not one damn bit. I'd known he would contact her, but as much as we needed to find him, I'd hoped that he wouldn't pull her into his shit. There was no reason for him to put her in danger. I couldn't believe that son of a bitch was planning on dragging her to that dump Lancaster's, but now that he was, I would do whatever it took to keep her safe.

Printed in Poland
by Amazon Fulfillment
Poland Sp. z o.o., Wrocław